'I expect you think I'm very peculiar,' said Pauline.

He shrugged. He had given up thinking women peculiar: they were just raving potty, the whole lot of them. What with Anita, who thought of nothing but the ballet, and now this one, wittering on about being peculiar –

'I *know* you think I'm peculiar,' she sa

'All right, then,   – who was he to cont   peculiar.'

'I knew you did.' Now she was happy. 'Men always do, but I can't help it . . . it's part of my insecurity thing.'

'What is?'

'The fact that I don't want to go back with them to have sex.'

Maybe she should have gone into a nunnery. Maybe they should all go into nunneries. It would be better than walking around inciting people – and anyway, no one had asked her to come back and have sex.

'All I was suggesting,' he said, 'was a coffee.'

JEAN URE has been writing full-time for the past twelve years, building up a well-deserved reputation as one of Britain's finest authors of fiction for young adults. YOU WIN SOME, YOU LOSE SOME is the first of her books to be published in Corgi Freeway.

YOU WIN SOME YOU LOSE SOME

JEAN URE

CORGI
F·R·E·E·W·A·Y

YOU WIN SOME, YOU LOSE SOME

A CORGI FREEWAY BOOK   0 552 52431 X

Originally published in Great Britain in 1984 by The
Bodley Head Ltd.

PRINTING HISTORY
Corgi Freeway edition published 1987

This book is set in 11/13 pt Century Schoolbook
by Colset Private Limited, Singapore.

Corgi Freeway Books are published by Transworld
Publishers Ltd., 61 – 63 Uxbridge Road, Ealing, London
W5 5SA, in Australia by Transworld Publishers
(Australia) Pty. Ltd., 15 – 23 Helles Avenue,
Moorebank, NSW 2170, and in New Zealand by
Transworld Publishers (N.Z.) Ltd., Cnr. Moselle and
Waipareira Avenues, Henderson, Auckland.

Made and printed in Great Britain by
Cox & Wyman Ltd., Reading, Berks.

You Win Some,
You Lose Some

1

'Leaving?' said Mr Loe. He frowned at Jamie across the cluttered acres of his desk. 'This is a bit sudden, Carter.' He leaned forward to peer at the pink folder in front of him. 'Carr. A bit sudden, isn't it? The Christmas term isn't when we normally expect our sixth-form pupils to depart from us.'

'No, sir. I s'pose it isn't, sir.'

'Do you have a job to go to?'

'Going to work in Plumber's, sir.'

'Plumbers? You mean —' The Head Master made vague, tap-turning motions with his hand.

'Big store, sir. Up in town.'

'Oh! That Plumber's; I see. Doing what, precisely?'

'Er — well —' Jamie hesitated. He wondered for a moment if he dared say 'Training to be a manager', or whatever it was one trained to be in big stores. That was the trouble: he wasn't really certain. He didn't know what people did in these places other than stand behind counters or pack things in basements.

'Mm?' Old Joe nodded at him, encouragingly.

'Packing,' said Jamie.

'Packing?'

'Packing and unpacking.'

One of Old Joe's eyebrows moved gently up into his receding hairline.

'Packing and unpacking ... Tell me — er — Carr. How many O levels did you —' He ran a bony finger down a sheet of paper inside the folder. 'Ah ... mm. Three CSEs. Grade C. Yes. Well —'

There was a pause. Old Joe closed the folder, and with it seemed to be closing the interview. He removed his bifocals and pinched the bridge of his nose between finger and thumb.

'I take it you have spoken to your house master about your intentions?'

Hell, thought Jamie. He shook his head, reluctant.

'No, sir.'

'No? Who is your house master?'

'Mr Hubbard.'

'Mr —?'

'Mr Hubbard.'

'Ah! Mr Hubbard. Yes, well, if I were you, er — Carr — I would go and have a word with Mr Hubbard and see what advice he is able to give you. He may possibly feel that in all the circumstances — but then again, of course, he may not. He, after all, is the one who best knows your capabilities. You go along to Mr Hubbard and see what he has to say.'

'Packing?' said the Hubbard. He leaned back in

his chair, feet comfortably propped on the edge of his desk, and flung a casual dart at the dart board stuck at the far side of the room on top of some bookshelves. The dart went wide and impaled itself in the wall. 'Damn!' said the Hubbard. He flung another. 'Packing what?'

'Dunno,' said Jamie.

'Packing gewgaws for the proles.'

Jamie blinked. The Hubbard flung his third dart: it landed quiveringly in the outer rim of the dart board.

'You realize, of course,' said the Hubbard, 'that I am farther away than two metres. Two metres —' he pointed — 'would be about there. This is more like three.' He strolled across, retrieved the darts, sank back again into his chair. 'So! You're walking out on us to go and become a packer.'

Wham! Wham! Wham! Three more darts embedded themselves in quick succession in the already pockmarked wall. The Hubbard snapped his fingers. Jamie, obediently, went across to retrieve.

'And ultimately?' said the Hubbard.

Ultimately?

'When the joys of packing start to fade ... what do we do then?' Wham! 'Operate the lifts for blue-rinsed dowagers? Flog electric tooth brushes? Put on a uniform and play at security guards?' Wham! Wham! 'Darts, please. — Thank you. — Doesn't sound very enthralling, does it?'

Jamie said nothing. It wasn't meant to be enthralling; it was just a job, to keep him going.

'What's the matter?' said the Hubbard. 'Brain gone to sleep?' He flung another dart: it landed with a triumphant thud in double twenty. 'There you are! See what a bit of persistence does? It's what I'm always trying to din into you people . . . *don't give up.*' He flung his remaining two darts: one went into the wall, one into the floor. 'Anyway,' said the Hubbard, tiring of the game, 'I would have thought you'd have had a bit more ambition.'

Jamie scowled. He had ambition; he just didn't see what business it was of the Hubbard's. He needn't think he was divulging his plans to *him*. He had suffered under the lash of the Hubbard's biting so-called wit quite long enough, he certainly wasn't laying himself open to yet another blast at this late stage.

'I'm here to tell you,' said the Hubbard, 'that you'll be bored stiff within a week. You may not be the world's number one intellect, but you're still a bright lad — well, save in the sphere of mathematics. There I think it can be said, without fear of contradiction, that you are without any doubt whatsoever a congenital cretin. You display a degree of ineptitude which in all my years I have rarely seen surpassed, other than by your friend Douglas. In all other respects, however, I would have said that your mental faculties functioned well above average.'

Jamie regarded him suspiciously. The Hubbard had once accused him of possessing the intellectual capacity of a three-toed sloth in a drug-induced coma: it was not the sort of remark that easily faded from the memory.

'I am aware,' conceded the Hubbard, 'that we have had our differences.'

He could say *that* again.

'You may not have shone in my particular subject, but that is far from saying you are equally moronic in others. I seem to recall your athletic prowess being not altogether undistinguished?'

Jamie made a vague, grunting noise; more of derision than assent. The Hubbard seemed surprised.

'No?'

'Well —'

He hunched a shoulder. His athletic prowess had come pretty much to a full stop, what with Bob Pearson chucking him out of the cricket eleven half way through last term, all because he'd refused to give the elbow to little old Miss Tucker and her dancing show, then him going and getting that pulled muscle only three matches into the soccer season. Miss Tucker had not been best pleased. She'd told him, straight out, 'If you're going to make a career as a dancer, you can't expect to go on disporting yourself on the football field. It must be one or the other, but not both. It's up to you; you must make your choice.' Somehow, by then, there had been only the one choice that he could make. He was in too deep to pull out — and in any case, what else was he capable of? With only three CSEs —

'You don't have to be Kevin Keegan,' said the Hubbard. 'There are other things you can usefully do with an aptitude for sport besides playing for England. How about teaching, for example? Ever thought of that?'

He thought of it now, and shuffled, uncomfortably. Who on earth, in their right minds, would want to TEACH? The Hubbard swung his feet off the desk.

'Jog my memory . . . what were your exam results like?'

'Lousy.'

'How lousy?'

'Dire-bolical.'

'O levels?'

'Nil.'

'Hm.' The Hubbard shook his head; regretfully, or so it seemed. (Could it be the guy actually *cared*?) 'All right, so you're not the academic type. That still doesn't mean you want to spend the next fifty odd years being bored out of your tree. There must be something you can do that gives you a buzz.'

There was a pause.

'Woodwork?' said the Hubbard.

Woodwork, metalwork, technical drawing. Come along, boy, you can't be that useless! How about tatting? How about —

'— dancing,' said the Hubbard. He shot out a paper knife in the shape of a dagger, pointing it accusingly at Jamie across the desk. 'Didn't I hear that you were in a show, or something? End of last term?'

If he hadn't, he must be about the only one. The Baboon and Roy Canary had not spared themselves in their efforts to spread the news.

'Someone said you had a real talent that way.'

12

The paper knife stabbed a couple of centimetres nearer. 'True?'

Jamie made another of his vague, grunting noises; more embarrassed, this time, than derisive. He ought never to have come and spoken to the Hubbard. It had simply been asking for trouble. With Old Joe you knew you were safe, because unless you'd managed to distinguish yourself in some way, such as setting fire to the school or winning some crapulous prize or other, the chances were he wouldn't know you from Adam. Old Joe was quite possibly the only person in the school who *hadn't* heard about Jamie being in Miss Tucker's show.

'So you can dance,' said the Hubbard.

He didn't deny it; he didn't see why he should. He was sick of denying things.

'And it gives you a buzz.'

Was that a question or a statement?

Question, obviously.

'Well, come on!' said the Hubbard. 'Does it or doesn't it? Stop being so hidebound! If you get a kick out of it, then why not say so?'

Jamie looked at him, stolidly, and said nothing. He wasn't setting himself up just to be knocked down again. He knew the Hubbard's tactics of old.

The Hubbard withdrew his paper knife.

'What's the problem? Kids been giving you a rough time?' He threw the knife, in apparent disgust, across the desk. 'Why is it you people are always so reactionary? Always so wrapped up in conventional attitudes? I suppose they've

13

already got you neatly labelled and docketed as one of the gay fraternity?'

A rash, bright crimson and resentful, broke out at the back of Jamie's neck. (*This*? From the *Hubbard*?)

'Look, all I'm trying to say,' said the Hubbard, 'is if you've found something you're good at, and it happens to be something you enjoy, then you hang on to it like grim death, because that, my lad, makes you one of the lucky ones. Most of your contemporaries are going to spend from now until they retire doing jobs that they loathe, or at the very best tolerate. So if you've found a way out, you take it.' He paused; made a steeple of his fingers and studied Jamie pensively a while over the top. 'Have you ever looked into the possibility of dancing as a career? Have you considered it?'

Jamie swallowed.

'Well, I —'

'Go away and think about it. Don't dismiss it out of hand. Above all, don't dismiss it simply because of a few cloth-eared cretins who have black holes where their brains ought to be. Never get anywhere if you listen to cloth-eared cretins.'

'No,' said Jamie.

He felt an idiot, now. He might just as well have come straight out with it, at the beginning — except how was he to know the Hubbard would turn out to be half-way human? He had never shown any signs of it before.

'All right,' said the Hubbard. He waved a hand. 'Off you go. Let me know what you decide.'

*   *   *

He already had decided; he had decided weeks ago. It had been the football match that had done it. Hobbling back to the changing room, afterwards, in agony from a pulled thigh muscle, and that great gormless idiot Forbes, whose only claim to distinction was the ability to crack all the joints of his fingers, one after another, leering at him from under the shower.

'That the leg you do your twirls on? Your bally teacher won't half be cross with you . . . playing a naughty rough game like football.'

Forbes was one of the Hubbard's cloth-eared cretins. Jamie didn't give a damn about Forbes, but he did give a damn about Miss Tucker. She hadn't been mad at him so much as coldly contemptuous. Scathingly she had said that if he thought it worth jeopardizing his entire future simply to gain a little temporary honour and glory kicking a football round a muddy field for ninety minutes a week, then that was up to him.

Somehow, it had put everything into perspective. All the jeers and the jibes, the dubious jests, even Doug's defection — when looked at in that light, they had faded into a sort of insignificance. Tenterden Road Comprehensive, when all was said and done, was but a phase: life beyond went on a great deal longer. The thought of spending it as some downtrodden minion on the shop floor was not one that appealed. As the Hubbard, so succinctly, had said: 'if you've found a way out, you take it.'

It had been Anita's idea that he should try for a

place at Kendra Hall. Carelessly, and not without a certain embarrassment (it was, let's face it, scarcely three months since he'd sworn blind that that was it, that was the end: he'd helped her out once, and never again) he'd put the suggestion to Miss Tucker. Perhaps even then, with one part of himself, the conventional, reactionary part that the Hubbard had railed about, he had subconsciously wanted her to reject it.

'My dear boy, just because you have the elementary ability to keep in time to a simple piece of music and not trip over your own feet, pray don't run away with the idea that you are cut out to be a professional.' (Miss Tucker set great store by being a professional.)

Perhaps if she had said that, he would have been secretly relieved. He could have stayed on at Tenterden and striven to redeem himself, to become once again one of the crowd. Unfortunately — or fortunately, he still couldn't quite decide — Miss Tucker hadn't said anything of the kind. Miss Tucker, in fact, had been every bit as enthusiastic as Anita.

'But of course you should try for a place! The sooner the better. If I'd realized you'd overcome your stupid prejudices, I'd have suggested it myself. Have you spoken to your parents?'

'Er — well — no,' he said. 'Not yet. I thought I ought to speak to you first.'

'That's right, get it settled. Present them with a *fait accompli*. Good idea.'

He wasn't quite sure what a fate accumply was, but whatever it was, if it meant postponing the moment when he had to break the news to his father he was all for it.

Miss Tucker, for her part, had wasted no time: before he knew it, she had him all fixed up for an audition the following Easter.

'Of course, you'll have to wait until the next September intake before you can actually start full-time, but that's no reason why you shouldn't enrol as a part-time student in the meanwhile. You could do that almost immediately. Let me see now, where is that prospectus . . . here we are! This is it . . . *Students may be admitted on a part-time basis prior to entering the school on a full-time course of study. Such students will be expected to attend classes on four nights per week plus Saturday mornings* . . . well, now!' She had fixed Jamie with one of her Gorgon-like gazes. 'I shouldn't think that would present any problems, would you?'

Other than the fact that it would take him over three hours to get there, all the way in by train to Liverpool Street, then all the way out again by tube to Ealing Broadway (eighteen stops, no less, on the Central Line) he agreed that it would present no problems at all: *he* didn't mind travelling six hours a day.

'Do I detect a note of sarcasm?' had said Miss Tucker, sharply. 'Pray do not be so foolish! You will do as Anita has done, and stay in Ealing. It will mean leaving school, of course, but from what you tell me that will be no great loss. It's not as if you're doing anything of importance. Nothing but free periods and pottery classes. No,

17

you'll be far better off getting out and seeing a bit of the world. Find yourself a job, that's the thing to do. Something temporary, just to tide you over . . . a bit of clerical work, or messengering.'

He had stared at her, in silent bemusement. A bit of clerical work, or messengering? Where had she been, all these years?

'Now what's the matter?' said Miss Tucker. 'You don't get anything for nothing, you know. Not in this life. You have to be prepared to work.'

'I'm prepared to work.' Him and a few million others. 'It's just that there's this little thing called unemployment.' He felt like adding, *you might have heard of it . . . there's quite a lot of it about*, only one didn't; not with Miss Tucker. 'It's not that easy. Most of the kids that left school the end of last term are still signing on.'

Miss Tucker dismissed most of the kids who had left school at the end of last term.

'They probably weren't motivated: you are. Where there's a will, there's always a way. You'll find something, if you look hard enough.'

When he mentioned it to Anita, on one of her weekends at home, she said, 'Oh, you don't want to worry about boring things like that! I'll talk to Daddy. He'll come up with something.'

That, of course, thought Jamie, was the real difference between him and the kids who had left school at the end of last term: they didn't have girl friends with rich daddies. (If Anita could be called a girl friend. It was a point he had never quite been able to decide. She was certainly a friend, and she was certainly a girl, but that

18

wasn't necessarily the same thing as being a girl friend. One of these days, when he was feeling bold, he really was going to have to put it to the test.)

The very next day, Anita had rung him.

'I've spoken to Daddy,' she said. 'He thinks he could get you something in one of his stores. You know they've got this branch at Ealing? Well, they have, and they're looking for someone to work down in the basement doing packing —' A sudden note of doubt had crept into her voice. 'You wouldn't *mind* doing packing, would you?'

'Don't mind what I do.' Anything was better than staying on at Tenterden — provided it was only temporary. He wouldn't want to do packing for the rest of his life.

'I said you wouldn't mind,' said Anita. 'After all, it's only a means to an end. Oh, and Mummy says that if you like she'll speak to Auntie Margaret and see if you could stay there with me during term time. Would you like her to?'

Jamie, at the other end of the telephone, hadn't quite known what to say. He'd never met Auntie Margaret, and Auntie Margaret had never met him, so how could he tell? Events were moving too fast. It was only a fortnight since he had come to his momentous decision and already they'd got him fixed up with an audition and a job, and now, it seemed, with digs as well. Not for the first time since falling within the orbit of Anita and Miss Tucker, he had the definite feeling of being bulldozed. Between the two of them, they were running his life for him — not that it was too late to back out even now.

'Look,' he could say, 'I've changed my mind. I've decided to stay on at school after all.'

Yes, and do what? Take a CSE in signing on? It always came back to the same problem: there was nothing he could actually *do*. He was just about as useless as that tergivisator, Doug. (He liked the word tergivisator. He'd found it in the dictionary, when he was looking for something else. It meant, 'to desert, to change one's allegiance': it fitted Doug exactly.)

Doug was spending his extra year at Tenterden smoking pot in the lavatories and screwing birds behind the bicycle sheds. Jamie couldn't even get to do that, though God knows it wasn't for want of trying. He'd taken out four girls so far this term and every single one of them had told him to keep his hands to himself. If it hadn't been for the fact that that useless, tergivisating, barrel-chested lump of moronity that had once passed as his best friend (*some friend*) was obviously having no trouble, he'd have been seriously tempted to condemn the female population of Tenterden as having something wrong with them. As it was, he supposed, glumly, that there must be something wrong with him. He presumably couldn't be approaching them right, though short of actually *paying* them —

He didn't have any money to pay people with. He never had had any money, and at this rate he never would. Working in Daddy's basement wasn't going to do much for the state of his finances. Just about buy him a daily bag of chips and cover the cost of his lodgings. He wondered, uneasily, how much Auntie Margaret was likely to want. If she wanted more than he was earning, then she could forget the idea, it didn't matter how nice she was. He was already going to have to ask his old man to fork out for lessons; he couldn't expect him to stump up with the rent as well.

'Oh, you won't have to pay *rent*,' said Anita, when she rang him back, as promised, the next morning. 'Auntie Margaret wouldn't dream of it. In any case, they've got more room than they know what to do with, specially when Toby and Babs are away.'

Toby and Babs? He felt the hairs at the back of his neck begin to prickle. Who on earth were Toby and Babs? (And what kind of a name was *Babs*, for heaven's sake?)

'Have you spoken to your parents yet, by the way?'

No; he hadn't. That embarrassment was still to come.

'I think you ought,' said Anita.

He knew he ought. He didn't need her telling him. Next thing he knew she'd be offering to do it for him.

He almost wished she would. At least his old man would listen to her without making any of his smart remarks. He could just imagine what his reaction was likely to be if *he* broke the news.

'Bally dancing? You can't take up bally dancing! Stone the flaming crows . . . next thing

21

I know you'll be wanting to flounce about the street wearing make-up!'

In the event, when finally, under pressure from Anita, he nerved himself to broach the subject, his father surprised him. After listening patiently to five minutes of Jamie, red and self-conscious, blethering his way through a list of prepared explanations — 'Even if I did stay on, it wouldn't get me anywhere. It's only a way of marking time. I mean, it's not as if I'm learning anything — it's not as if I'm going to take any more exams or anything. If I were going to take exams it might be different. But all we do is have free periods and mess around. I mean —'

'All right, lad. All right.' Mr Carr held up a conciliatory hand. 'No need to work yourself into a lather. I get the message: you've had a bellyful of school, and you want out. So, that's fair enough. I've got nothing to say against that. As to this dancing lark — well, it's not what I'd have chosen, and I won't pretend it is, but if you think it's what you want —' He shrugged, evidently determined to be broad-minded. 'I suppose there are worse things you could do.'

Dead right there were worse things he could do! Like flogging himself half to death running someone's lousy off-licence for them. He was on the point of saying so, when Mr Carr said it for him:

'At least it'll be better than humping crates of booze for a living, I'll grant you that. You go ahead, lad, and give it a bash. It seems you've some sort of a talent that way, so you might as well make use of it. I'm not sure how I'll break it to the customers —' He grinned, just to show that he was joking, but Jamie knew that he wasn't; not altogether. 'Still, I daresay we shall manage to live it down. Wait till you're on the telly, giving it the old one, two.' Mr Carr doubled his fists and took a couple of swipes at an imaginary opponent. 'That'll be the day!'

For some time afterwards, whenever he thought about the step that he was taking — step that he was being *pushed* into taking: he blamed it all on Anita and Miss Tucker — Jamie had this vision of Mr Carr with his fists doubled up, swinging punches at an imaginary foe. It seemed to him that it was his father's way of saying what he couldn't say out loud: I wish to God you'd picked on something I could understand and sympathize with, instead of something I have to make excuses for . . .

His mother, when he told her, said: 'Well, and I don't blame you. Good for you. I don't expect your father approves, but never you mind about him. It's your life, not his. Anyway, he'll come round to it, given time. You have a go, that's what I say.'

Kim, of course, was in ecstasies. He hadn't wanted her to know, but Mrs Carr had told him not to be so silly.

'You can't keep a thing like that from your own sister!'

It wasn't keeping it from Kim that bothered him so much as Kim keeping it from everyone else. In his experience, entrusting that kid with a secret was like entrusting a monkey with a bag of nuts: self-control simply flew out of the window.

'You're not to tell anyone,' he said. 'Right?'

Kim made her eyes go big; an annoying female habit she had recently acquired.

'But *Jamie, why*?'

'Because I say so, that's why! I don't want anyone to know, and I mean *anyone*.'

'Not even at school?'

'Especially not even at school.' Not, at any rate, until he was safely out of it. He didn't fancy the idea of his life being made a misery for the last six weeks. 'You just keep it to yourself if you don't want to wake up with your throat cut.'

'Couldn't I just tell Karen?'

'No, you could not just tell Karen! I said not to tell *anyone*.'

'But Karen goes to Miss Tucker's.'

'I don't care where she goes! You breathe so much as a word to a single soul and you're for it. Do I make myself clear?'

Kim pouted.

'I don't see why I can't just tell Karen.'

'Because I've told you not just to tell Karen! I want your word on it.'

'What word?'

'Any word — just so long as you stick to it.'

'Oh, all *right*.' Grudgingly, Kim licked her right forefinger. 'Cross my heart and hope to die, go to hell if I tell a lie . . . not that I *believe* it.'

'You'd better,' said Jamie.

2

He had always imagined that the day he left school would be in some way momentous; it turned out, instead, to be a total non-event. He went in for Assembly, sat through Old Joe's usual end-of-term homily, joined in the usual end-of-term dirge ('Lord dismiss us with thy blessing,' or 'Thank the Lord we're free to go now', as he and Doug, in the old days, had used to sing, honking away together like a pair of tone-deaf geese) and finally he filed out again, unmoved and indifferent, to the usual end-of-term Beatles medley, which was Old Joe's concession to what he called 'the callow taste of unformed youth'.

Once Assembly was over, there really wasn't much point in hanging around. (It occurred to him that there really hadn't been much point in coming in at all.) He went back upstairs to the Sixth Year common room, opened his locker, removed a couple of old T-shirts and a pair of trainers, left the rest of the rubbish for the scavengers to pick over after he was gone, and that was that, five and a bit years of Tenterden Comprehensive over and done with as if it had never been. He didn't even bother saying good-bye to anyone, just stuffed his things into his bag and walked out. On his way past the staff room he was stopped by the Hubbard, who wished him good luck and told him that he was going to miss his dumb and cretinous presence in his maths class next term.

'You have a certain down-to-earth sanity which I confess has periodically lightened my darkness.'

It scarcely seemed a very fitting epitaph for one who had, in his time, been called a disruptive element.

On Boxing Day he had been invited round to Anita's to meet Auntie Margaret. 'Come round about three,' Anita had said, but at quarter to the Carrs were still sitting round the kitchen table mopping up the remnants of yesterday's Christmas pudding. Jamie pushed his plate away.

'I'd better be off now,' he said.

'Have you got Anita's present?'

Of course he had Anita's present. It was in his jacket pocket, all neatly done up for him by Kim in fancy wrapping paper.

'How about the wine?'

'The wine's outside.'

He had left it outside on purpose. In expansive mood, on Christmas Eve, Mr Carr had told him to help himself to whatever he wanted, so he had done just that and taken champagne. With any luck, by the time its loss was discovered (if ever it was) it would be put down to shoplifters.

'Off you go, then,' said Mrs Carr. 'Have a good time.'

He went outside and picked up his bottle. He felt like a kid going to a party —' Off you go, then. Have a good time.'

He was only going round there to meet Auntie Margaret.

He slopped across the Common, through the yellowing mush of the pre-Christmas snow, clutching his bottle protectively to his chest as if even now Mr Carr might scent malpractice and come galloping after him. Not that there was much likelihood, seeing as it was his custom, after Boxing Day dinner, to go and snore his head off in front of the television. He wondered what Anita's parents would be doing. Something rich and gracious, like eating caviare or sorting the family jewels; certainly not snoring their heads off in front of television sets or sitting at tables full of dirty dishes.

He arrived promptly at three o'clock and rang the bell. (He was always surprised it wasn't one of the ding-dong sort that played tunes. You'd have thought, what with Daddy being a sales director, or whatever he was, they could have run to something a bit different. All they had was an ordinary buzzing thing, though admittedly it did light up in the dark.)

The door was answered by a fattish, freckled child about the same age as Kim. She looked up at him from beneath a thatch of straw-coloured hair.

'Are you Jamie?' she said.

'Yes,' he said. 'Who're you?'

'I'm Babs.' Self-important, she held open the door. 'You'd better come in.'

He did so, carefully wiping his feet on the mat. The child stood watching him.

'Everyone's asleep,' she said.

He was startled.

'Everyone?'

'Well, not *every*one . . . Anita's not. And Toby's not.' She closed the door behind him. 'They're in there.'

She conducted him through to Anita's studio. In the centre of the room Anita was standing, with a long, lanky boy who must presumably be Toby.

'He's come,' said Babs.

'So we see,' said the boy.

Anita stepped forward. She was wearing a pink velvety pinafore dress with a blouse covered all over in little pink flowers, and had her hair hanging loose about her shoulders. He'd never seen Anita with her hair like that before, it was always screwed into a bun or scraped back with an elastic band. He felt suddenly bashful, and didn't know what to say.

'This is Toby,' said Anita.

'Hi, there,' said Toby.

He was probably about the same age as Jamie, but one of the suave, sophisticated type. You could tell he was suave and sophisticated just looking at him. He had a long, narrow face with limp hair the colour of old dish rags which fell forward into his eyes, and which he casually flicked out again with a finger as long and narrow

28

as his face. The sort who could pass exams without even trying and had sports cars given him for his birthday.

'We were just talking about going out to get some air,' said Anita.

Toby picked up a stripy scarf.

'Counteract the effects of a surfeit of gastronomic indulgence.'

It was exactly the sort of remark that you would expect a person who wore stripy scarves to make.

'Everyone else,' explained Anita, 'has gone to sleep.'

Toby looped his scarf elegantly about his neck.

'That, you understand, is a polite way of putting it. Sunk in swinish slumber would be a more apt description . . . the liquid refreshment, as you might say, has done for them.'

Talking of liquid refreshment reminded him. He held out his bottle.

'I brought this,' he said.

'Cor, luv a duck!' It was Toby who snatched it from him. 'A bottle of Moët . . . that'll go down a treat!'

'Also —' he fished in his pocket — 'I bought this for you.'

'For me?' A spot of pink appeared in Anita's cheek. 'What is it?'

'Why not try opening it,' drawled Toby, 'and see?'

'I hate opening things in front of people.' She hesitated; looking across, rather anxiously, at Jamie. 'Can I leave it till later?'

'I don't mind,' he said. To tell the truth, he'd just as soon she did. He still wasn't convinced that a brooch in the shape of a dancer had been the right thing to get her. Kim had approved, but then Kim wasn't necessarily anything to go by: she'd spent the whole of last term nagging to have green stripes put in her hair. You couldn't really rely on someone who fancied herself with green stripes.

'Look, now that he's *here*,' said Babs, 'why can't we go?'

They set off across the Common, Toby and Anita leading the way, Jamie following behind with Babs. He supposed it was only natural that a person would rather not have to be stuck with his own kid sister, but he could have wished they'd all kept together instead of splitting up. *He* didn't know what to talk to the wretched child about. He ransacked his brains for some topic of conversation.

'What kind of a name is Babs?' he said.

'Don't you know?' She looked up at him; surprised and contemptuous. 'It's short for Barbara.'

'Is it?' He hadn't known. How was he supposed to know? He'd never met anyone called Babs. Come to think of it, he'd never met anyone called Barbara, either. He cast around for something else. 'Jamie's short for James,' he said.

'I know that.' Now she sounded scornful. 'Everybody knows that.'

Yes, he supposed they did. It was pretty obvious.

'Sometimes it's shortened to Jim,' he said; and then quickly, before she could inform him that she knew that, as well: 'Or even Jimbo.'

'Jimbo's American,' said Babs.

He looked down at her, stumping by his side in big, red, shiny gumboots.

'How old are you?'

'Nearly eleven. How old are you?'

'Nearly seventeen,' said Jamie.

If he'd thought she'd be impressed, he was wrong.

'Toby's nearly nineteen. He's at university.'

Of course, thought Jamie; he would be, wouldn't he?

'What's he studying?'

'He's not studying,' said Babs. 'He's reading.'

'So what's he reading?' He felt like saying 'Girly mags?' but thought perhaps he'd better not. Tamely, he substituted: 'Noddy books?'

'Hist'ry,' said Babs.

Hist'ry. That sounded like an easy life. Anyone could just sit down and read a bit of hist'ry. You didn't need any sort of a brain to do that.

'You're going to go to Anita's ballet school,' said Babs. She said it as if it were something he didn't know about; as if it were a decision that had been made over his head. (Which in some ways it had.) 'My brother —' She paused, and they both gazed ahead at Toby, walking with Anita. He had his shoulders hunched against the wind, and both hands jammed into the pockets of his commando-style jacket. 'My brother,' said Babs, 'says that all men that dance are bum bandits.'

Jamie swallowed, and choked.

'He says they're *what*?'

'Bum bandits.'

There was a silence. Jamie stared venomously at the hunch-backed figure in its commando-style jacket. So Toby said that all men that danced were bum bandits, did he?

'What *is* a bum bandit?' said Babs.

'Not telling you.'

'Why not?' She looked up at him, aggrieved, from beneath a frizzy fringe of hair.

'Because I'm not.'

'Why? Is it something rude?'

Prudishly he said: 'It's something you oughtn't to be talking about.'

'Then it *is* something rude. I s'pose it's like saying tit and prick.'

Toby was a prick; great stringy academic beanpole. Just let him get him into a quiet corner and he'd show him a thing or two. He'd —

'Well, *is* it?' said Babs, growing impatient.

'Is what what?'

'Is bum bandit like saying tit and prick?'

For crying out loud!

'You don't have to shout,' he said.

'Then tell me!'

'No.'

She scowled.

'I can always find out . . . I've already read all the dirty bits in *Lady Chatterley*.'

At eleven years old? He was outraged. What were these kids coming to? At eleven years old he hadn't even *heard* of *Lady Chatterley*.

'If you want to know as badly as all that,' he said, 'why don't you try asking your brother?'

'*He* won't tell me.'

'Well, considering he said it to you —'

'He didn't say it to me. He said it to Anita.'

'I see.' He glared with renewed venom at the Hunchback. It had now removed its hands from its pockets and was beating its arms across its weedy chest — if chest it could be called. The guy simply wouldn't stand a chance; he'd be mashed to a pulp. People with chests like that ought to be a bit more careful, the things they went round accusing people of. They could get themselves into a whole lot of trouble. 'What did —' he strove to keep his voice casual — 'what did Anita say?'

'Not going to tell you,' said Babs.

He looked down at her with dislike: obnoxiousness obviously ran in the family.

'If you want to know,' she said, 'you can ask Anita.'

'What a very unpleasant little girl you are,' said Jamie.

She tossed her frizzy fringe.

'Why should I tell you what you want to know if you won't tell me what I want to know?'

'Because what you want to know isn't good for you to know.' He was talking like a parent. Why shouldn't he tell her what she wanted to know? What the hell did it matter? She was going to discover sooner or later. And anyway, if she really *had* read all the dirty bits in *Lady Chatterley* — 'OK,' he said. 'I'll strike a bargain. You tell me what Anita said, then I'll tell you what you want to know.'

'I want to know what a bum bandit is.'

'Yeah, OK! OK!' He made shushing motions with his hand: they weren't the only people out walking on the Common. There were respectable people there, as well. People with eleven-year-old kids who *hadn't* read *Lady Chatterley*. 'Tell me what Anita said first.'

'And then you'll tell me what a b —'

'I just said so, didn't I?'

'All right. But if you don't, I'll tell Anita. I'll tell her you wanted to know what she —'

'Look, just shut up,' he said, 'and get on with it. Tell me what she said.'

'She said she didn't care what people were so long as they could dance. She said being able to dance was the only thing that matters.'

In spite of himself, Jamie found a slow grin starting to spread across his face. Trust Anita. *Being able to dance was the only thing that matters* . . . that must have been one in the eye for the Hunchback.

'Now it's your turn,' said Babs.

'Yeah —' He hesitated. This was not going to be so easy. How in heaven's name was one supposed to explain to an eleven-year-old, even if it had read *Lady Chatterley*? He cleared his throat. 'Well,' he said. 'It's like this . . . you know what a bandit is?' She nodded. 'And you know what a bum is. Well —'

He stopped.

'I'll tell Anita!' said Babs.

'All right! All right!' He shushed her again. 'I'm getting there.' It wasn't something you could just launch into, without any preparation. He didn't want to be accused, later in life, of having warped her. 'Look,' he said. 'You know what dogs sometimes get up to when there's a lady dog around and it's got them all excited?'

'No,' said Babs. 'What?'

Jesus! This was going to be hard work. He tried again.

'What about the zoo?' he said. 'Now, you must have been to the zoo . . .'

They arrived back to find that the soporific effects of too much liquid refreshment had worn off, and that the aged P.s, as the Hunchback referred to them, were all awake and rarin' to go. Daddy was eager for some amusement, so after Jamie had been introduced to Auntie Margaret (almost a twin version of Mummy, who was, in her turn, an older version of Anita) and to Uncle Richard (big and bruising, unlike the Hunchback) they all had to sit round and think of games to play.

'Why don't we do charades?' said Mummy.

'Oh, yes! Let's!' said Auntie Margaret.

The Hunchback and Anita exchanged glances. The Hunchback rolled his eyes: Anita very faintly shrugged her shoulders.

'We always do charades,' said Babs.

'And why shouldn't we?' said Auntie Margaret. 'It's better than sitting gawping at the television all day. Now, how shall we split up?'

'You and Andrew,' said Mummy, 'and me and Richard.'

'I'm not doing it with Babs,' said the Hunchback.

No, thought Jamie; neither was he. He was none too sure what this charades thing entailed, but whatever it was he wasn't doing it with that child. He wasn't doing *any*thing with that child. Not after the embarrassment she'd put him through, out there on the Common.

'Oh, I *see*,' she'd said, after he'd gone through practically every zoo animal he could think of. 'You mean they're homo*sex*ual.' She'd not only yelled it at the top of her voice, but had dragged the word out as far as it would go —' ho-mo--*sex*-ual' — lovingly lingering over each syllable. The Hunchback and Anita, some hundred yards away, had both stopped dead and turned to stare.

'We'll take Babs,' said Mummy. 'You can go with Margaret and Andrew.'

Andrew, presumably, must be Daddy. Mummy, he knew, was Christine, because he'd heard Daddy call her by that name. The Hunchback was looking peeved.

'What about Anita?'

'Anita can go with Jamie. They can do one together.'

The Hunchback, at that, looked even more peeved. Anita leaned across to whisper in Jamie's ear.

'I'm sorry about this — they *always* want to do it. I think it must take them back to their childhood, or something.'

36

'Stop whispering,' said Mummy, 'it's very rude. If you and Jamie have secrets you can discuss them together later, when you do your word. Who's going to go first? Shall we?'

Mummy and Uncle Richard left the room, accompanied by a resigned-looking Babs. The Hunchback said, 'God! I hope they don't do prestidigitator again.'

'They did that last year,' said Anita.

'I know they did. It took for ever.'

'Toby, come over here,' said Auntie Margaret. 'We need you. We're going to discuss our word.'

With bad grace, the Hunchback took himself over to the far side of the room. Jamie and Anita were left together on the sofa.

'When we go outside,' said Anita, 'I'll open your present. I've got one for you, as well, but I didn't want to give it to you in front of Toby.'

He was glad about that. Perhaps it meant she felt the same way about the Hunchback as he did.

Mummy and her team came back into the room. Mummy was wearing a lampshade on her head and had a silk bedspread draped about her shoulders. Uncle Richard had removed his jacket and opened his shirt right down as far as his waist, revealing a chest full of hairs (he bet the Hunchback didn't have hairs) and had tied what looked like a tea-towel round his middle. Babs stepped forward and said: 'This is the first syllabub and I'm a conductor.'

'Bus conductor?' said the Hunchback.

'No, you idiot, a *musical* conductor.'

They did a scene in which Babs stood and

waved her arms about and Mummy and Uncle Richard sang a snatch from some opera or other (' "Carmen",' said Anita. 'It's *always* "Carmen" ') and then broke off to conduct a fierce quarrel in a mixture of foreign languages. After that they all trooped out again and everyone began to discuss what the syllable could have been.

'Isn't it *hell*?' said Anita.

Jamie tried to look as though it was, since she and the Hunchback seemed to be in agreement on the point, but in fact he had quite enjoyed seeing Mummy dressed up in a lampshade and Uncle Richard in his tea-towel. For their next scene they were school children, with Uncle Richard in a pair of running shorts and Mummy in a mini skirt, showing all her legs. (Anita groaned: 'She does that *every year*.')

'If you ask me, it's going to be mongoose,' said Daddy.

'Mongoose?' said Auntie Margaret. 'How can it be mongoose? *I* say it's going to be something beginning with per ... perchance, perhaps, perform —'

As it turned out the word wasn't any of those things, it was basket. Daddy said: 'I didn't hear anyone say bask.'

'It was all that filthy foreign gibberish,' said the Hunchback. 'It threw us.'

Mummy looked pleased.

'It was meant to.' She clapped her hands. 'Go on, then! Your turn.'

Daddy and Auntie Margaret leapt for the door,

the Hunchback, with an air of martyrdom, trailing after.

'I s'pose we ought to be thinking of a word,' said Anita.

Jamie looked around, at the Christmas decorations.

'Mistletoe?' he said.

'*Any*thing, so long as it's not prestidigitator.'

Daddy and Auntie Margaret came back. They didn't go in so much for dressing themselves up in lampshades and miniskirts (the Hunchback didn't go in for anything at all, but merely slunk about in the background looking superior): they tended to favour scenes of heavy drama. Daddy was a bit of a clown, in an unintentional sort of way. He kept muffing his words and tripping over bits of furniture, and once he went down on his knees and got part of his shoe wedged beneath a chair and couldn't get back up again. Jamie thought perhaps it might have something to do with the large bubble of brandy from which he constantly refreshed himself.

'Isn't it chronic?' said Anita.

'What's the word?' Mummy wanted to know. 'What's the word?'

Anita humped a shoulder; Uncle Richard lit up a big cigar.

'Penguin?' suggested Jamie.

'Do you think so?' Mummy sounded doubtful.

'How can it be penguin?' said Anita. 'You can't have guin.'

It wasn't penguin, but pensive.

'There!' said Mummy. 'You got the first syllable right, Jamie.'

The Hunchback looked at him, sneeringly.

'Now it's the lovebirds,' said Daddy. 'Off you go!' He shooed Jamie and Anita off the couch and sank down in their place. 'Don't take too long about it or we shall begin to wonder what you're up to.'

They left the room, amidst general titters of adult laughter.

'*Parents*,' said Anita.

He knew what she meant.

'Let's go in here.' She took his arm and pulled him through into the studio. 'I'll go and get my present — and my one for you.'

The present she had bought for him was a book called *Famous Male Dancers*.

'I thought you ought to read it,' she said. 'Just in case you're still having doubts.'

'About what?'

'Well, you know . . . about whether it's right.'

'Oh! That!' He assumed an air of unconcern. 'I've given up on that.'

'Well, it was a bit out of date,' said Anita. 'I mean, it's not as if anyone really *cares*. Not these days. Anyone can be anything they like, these days. Being able to dance is the only thing that — oh!' She had removed the wrapping from the ballet-dancer brooch. 'A brooch!'

'Is it OK?' he said.

'It's super! It'll go with my collection. Shall I put it on straight away?'

He made a mumbling noise.

'If you like.'

'I think I ought. After all, it is a present . . . do

40

you want to pin it on for me?'

He approached her, awkwardly.

'Where shall I pin it?'

'Here,' said Anita. She patted the area directly above her left breast.

He wasn't very good at this sort of thing at the best of times — pinning things on people, fastening zips, tying hair ribbons; it always made him all fingers and thumbs. Gingerly, trying to avoid too much personal contact in case she didn't like it, he slid a hand beneath the neck of her pink velvety dress. He remembered, last term, trying to grope Sharon out on the Common and Sharon slapping his face for him. He swallowed — and realized, too late, that he wasn't just holding her dress but her blouse as well.

'Sorry,' he said.

'That's all right,' said Anita.

'Did I —' He was about to say, 'prick you?' but suddenly the word had lost all innocent connotations and had but the one, unmistakable, meaning. On the spur of the moment he couldn't think of another to replace it. 'Did I —'

'No,' said Anita.

'Ah.' He swallowed again. Odd that when he was dancing with her he could touch her without any stronger sensation than mild pleasure, whereas now, when he wasn't even being particularly intimate —

There was a sudden bang on the door and the Hunchback's head appeared.

'Aren't you ready yet? Everyone's getting tired of waiting.'

41

Jamie stepped back a pace. Anita rearranged the neck of her pinafore dress.

'We're just coming.'

'Well, so long as you are — before your guv'nor gets boozed to the eyeballs.'

The Hunchback disappeared again.

'I've forgotten what we were going to do,' said Anita.

'Mistletoe.'

'Oh, yes. Missal and toe. Toe's easy — you can be a ballet master, giving me a lesson. I don't know about missal . . . what *is* a missal?'

'Dunno,' said Jamie. 'Kind of bird, isn't it?'

'You mean, like a mistlethrush? I s'pose that'd do. We could be walking through some woods and listening to the birds and you could say "What's that?" and I could say "That's a mistlethrush" . . . something like that. And then we'll do toe. And then when we get to the last one —'

'We can be walking through some more woods and I can say "What's that?" and you can say, "That's mistletoe".'

Anita giggled.

'Why not?'

The first scene they did lasted for about half a minute. The second, which was the ballet class, got a bit out of hand and went on for more like a quarter of an hour, in spite of Jamie managing to slip in the word 'toe' right at the beginning.

'Do you think they've guessed?' said Anita.

'Shouldn't think so,' said Jamie. 'We only said mistlethrush about ten times.'

'*Twice*,' said Anita. 'And anyway, we mentioned lots of other things as well.'

'Yeah, like sparrow hawks and kestrels ... they're just likely to be the first syllable of anything.'

When they went back into the sitting room to act the final scene, they found that someone had strategically suspended a piece of mistletoe directly above the acting area. It dangled in front of their faces, hanging by a thread of tinsel from the lamp shade. Steadfastly, they ignored it.

'Final scene,' said Anita. 'Wood, as before.'

She linked her arm through Jamie's and they walked in a circle, discussing birdsong, finally coming to a halt beneath the lampshade.

'What's that, then?' said Jamie, pointing.

'That's mistletoe,' said Anita.

Babs gave a triumphant shriek.

'We knew it was mistletoe! We knew all along!'

The Hunchback rolled his eyes: Mummy and Auntie Margaret politely applauded.

'That's surely not the end of it?' said Daddy. 'What d'you think we stuck the mistletoe up there for?'

Anita looked at it, and blushed.

'Silly word to choose,' observed the Hunchback, 'if you didn't intend to take advantage of it.'

Jamie also looked up at the mistletoe. It had never occurred to him; it honestly hadn't. He glanced anxiously at Anita, wondering if she would believe it. He wouldn't like her to think it had been part of some diabolical plot.

'Come on, then, Jamie!' That was Uncle Richard, joining in the fun. 'You know what mistletoe's for, don't you? Give the girl a kiss!'

'And make it a good one,' said Daddy. 'None of your quick pecks.'

They looked at each other.

'Well, go on,' grumbled the Hunchback. 'Get it over with.'

Anita tipped her face up: Jamie leaned forward.

'Hip, hip!' shouted Daddy.

A cheer went up from the assembled company: 'Hooray!'

'Lord preserve us,' muttered the Hunchback.

3

'OK, everyone! Five-minute break. Take it easy — but don't go all to pieces.'

Jamie staggered thankfully to the side of the room, wobbling on legs like semolina pudding. His muscles had turned all to jelly: his hair, when he touched it, was wringing wet. He had thought little old Miss Tucker was a slave driver, but she was as nothing compared with this guy — BEN Bregonzi, or whatever his name was. This guy was something else. A cross between the Marquis de Sade and Attila the Hun.

'You'll probably have Mr Bregonzi,' Anita had said. 'All the boys have Mr Bregonzi ... he's super.'

How she could say that he was super when he was barely a metre and a half tall and looked like an ageing spider monkey, Jamie couldn't imagine, but he had long since learnt that there was no accounting for girls' tastes: they picked on the most unlikely of specimens.

He slung his towel round his neck and slowly slumped down on to the floor, back pressed against the wall. All the other five members of

the class were doing likewise, save for one boy
who had been called over to talk to Ben Bregonzi.
Jamie gazed at him, covertly, across the studio.
His name was Brett Hamilton — he had introduced himself, in ringing tones, in the canteen
before class. He had bright yellow hair and had
arrived wearing scarlet leg warmers over his
jeans. Jamie wasn't too sure about Brett
Hamilton. He wasn't too sure about Percy
Winston Woo, either. Percy came from Hong
Kong and was very small, rather pretty, and
spoke with a bit of a lisp, which might or might
not have been due to the fact of his being foreign.
On the whole, whichever it was, he wasn't the
sort of person one would care to be seen out in the
street with; not, at any rate, by any of the thugs
from Tenterden.

All the other three — a black guy called Errol
May, a white guy called Steven Bothwell, and a
nondescript type called Graham Something-or-
Other — looked mercifully quite normal. All,
apart from the flamboyant Brett, were wearing
regulation black tights with black or white T-
shirts. Brett's T-shirt was scarlet, to go with his
scarlet leg warmers, which he wore defiantly over
vomit-green tights. From the way Ben Bregonzi
was rapping him about various portions of his
anatomy with his stick, Jamie gathered that his
choice of colour scheme was coming in for criti-
cism. Hardly surprising. It had stated, quite
plainly, in the letter of acceptance, that boys
should wear black tights for classes.

'All right, you lot!' Ben Bregonzi stopped

rapping at the scarlet leg warmers and rapped instead upon the piano. 'That's enough lazing around. On your feet — let's be having you!'

Steven Bothwell groaned and pulled a face.

'There surely must be easier ways of life than this?'

'Yeah, like coal heaving,' said Jamie, 'for instance.'

Percy Winston Woo, already up and on his feet, extended a dainty helping hand.

'You pass second wind, all be well.'

'Not if they pass it near me it won't be,' said Errol.

Percy looked at him, puzzled. 'Please?'

Ben Bregonzi's stick rapped again: it was growing impatient.

'Get a move on, over there, and stop gassing! Like a load of old women! What do you think this is? A bingo session?'

By the time the class came to an end, sharp on the dot of eight-thirty, Jamie was almost beginning to wish that it were. He was going to pay for this tomorrow; already, the thought of humping crates was an agony. He glanced round at the others and saw that they were all, in some degree or another, sharing his suffering. Brett had actually at some stage removed his leg warmers. Only the diminutive Percy appeared unruffled and unmarked.

'Tonight,' said Ben Bregonzi, 'I have let you off lightly — seeing it was your first class. Tomorrow I shall expect everyone to put in just that little bit more effort. By the end of the week —' he paused, to let it sink in — 'by the end of the week I intend that we shall start working.'

The boys' evening class was the last one of the day. By the time they had finished changing it was almost nine o'clock and the place deserted; the canteen had closed an hour ago, the various studios stood empty and in darkness. Only Ben Bregonzi still remained. He stood talking to the caretaker, who was waiting, keys in hand, in the entrance hall, ready to lock up.

'Don't forget!' he called after them, cheerfully. 'A bit of extra effort tomorrow.'

'If we can still move,' grumbled Brett.

He had put his leg warmers on again, plus an embroidered sheepskin coat adorned with fringes. He was at least colourful, thought Jamie; you had to grant him that. He personally wouldn't have been seen dead in a coat adorned with fringes, but he supposed there was no harm in it. It wasn't really something you could hold against a person. He was glad, all the same, that it was Steven who had chosen to walk with him, and not Brett.

'Which way are you headed? Common, or Broadway?'

'Common,' said Jamie. 'Which way are you?'

'Doesn't really matter; either suits me. I'll go to the Common, if that's the way you're going. — Anyone else coming our way?'

It seemed that all the others went to Ealing Broadway. They accordingly parted company at the school gates, Jamie and Steven turning left, the others continuing straight on.

'Feel like stopping off somewhere for a quick one?' said Steven.

The suggestion put him on the spot. He didn't like to say that he wasn't in the habit of stopping off for quick ones. He and Doug *had* occasionally downed the odd half pint, nicked from the shelves of the Carrs' off-licence, but the only time they'd ever attempted to enter a pub they'd been booted out as if they were vermin. Doug had blamed Jamie, for not looking older. That had been back at the start of the summer, almost seven months ago, but privately he had doubts whether he'd pass for eighteen even now. If he'd started shaving it would help. He inspected his chin regularly for any signs of growth, but as yet there didn't appear to be even so much as a hint of preliminary fluff.

He stole a quick look at Steven, as they passed beneath a street lamp. Impossible to make out, in its jaundiced yellow glow, whether Steven had started shaving, but he certainly had about him the enviable air of one who could enter a public house without suffering the humiliation of being told to remove himself.

Steven turned his head. He was a few centimetres taller than Jamie, but there wasn't much in it. They were of similar sort of build.

'So . . . how about it?'

Jamie shook his head; not without regret.

'I reckon I ought to go straight in and hit the sack. I've got a pretty heavy day tomorrow.'

'Still at school?' said Steven.

At least he was able to give the right answer to

that. He explained that he had left school last term and was working in the basement at Plumber's, just to tide him over.

'What's it like?' said Steven.

'Not bad.'

It was boring, more than anything. Once you'd packed (or unpacked) one crate full of china and glassware and humped it in or out of the service lift you'd experienced just about everything the job had to offer. His workmates weren't of the brightest. There was Charlie, who was in charge, because Charlie had been in basements longer than anyone else; then there was Big Mac, who was a thwarted lift man — 'They said I wouldn't do, on account of my height . . . you have to be small, for the lifts'; and there was Dennis, whose ambition it was to get into the basement in Oxford Street, Oxford Street being considered a step up from Uxbridge Road, Ealing. There'd been a few ribald remarks when they'd heard Jamie was taking ballet lessons, but it had all been perfectly good-natured. Now, if anything, they tended to treat him as a mascot.

'This is our little Fred Astaire,' they'd say, every time anyone new appeared in the basement. 'Goin' to bally school to be a bally dancer.'

He didn't mind the occasional bit of leg-pulling, he could stand that; it was the thought that some people got stuck packing crates for the whole of their working lives that depressed him.

'I guess it's OK,' he said, 'as a temporary measure.' As a temporary measure he felt that he could even grow quite fond of them all; just so

50

long as he knew there was an escape route. 'How about you?' he said. 'You working, or —'

'Got a job in a bookshop. Up in town. Doesn't pay much, but it has certain perks.'

He wondered what perks you could get, working in a bookshop. A free read, he supposed, if you happened to like books.

They turned off the road, on to the Common. It was small, compared to the one at home; hardly any more than a scrubby bit of green.

Steven said: 'I suppose you're living with your folks?'

'Mm-mm.' He made a negative noise in the back of his throat. 'Staying with people.'

'Digs?'

'Not exactly.' He explained about Auntie Margaret being Anita's mother's sister, and how they had this big house with more room than they knew what to do with.

'Handy,' said Steven. 'I've got this place in Hammersmith — well, I call it a place. Actually, it's more like a cupboard — more like a hole in the wall. Still, at least I can do what I like there.'

'This is it,' said Jamie. He had no doubt that if he really wanted, he could do what he liked at Auntie Margaret's. She was very liberal. There weren't any rules or regulations — no one said that he had to be in by a certain time, or telephone his movements, or anything like that. He just didn't somehow feel quite comfortable.

'I wouldn't mind a place of my own,' he said.

'I'll keep an eye open. Let you know if anything turns up.'

They walked on for a while in silence. It was quite an amiable silence; nothing awkward or constrained about it. Usually, when confronted with a void, Jamie found himself assailed by the desperate need to say something — anything — no matter how ludicrous or inapposite. He knew he was no great conversationalist, for Doug had once told him so. 'You know your trouble, don't you?' he'd said. 'You haven't got any conversation, that's your trouble.' Looking back on it, he almost began to wonder what he'd ever seen in Doug. It wasn't as if they'd ever had anything particularly in common.

'Tell me,' said Steven. 'You going to take this lot up for real?'

'What? You mean —'

'The ba*llay*,' said Steven, pronouncing it like an American. 'You really aiming to do it seriously?'

'Aren't you?' He'd assumed, automatically, that they all were. He must be catching Anita's bug — taking it for granted that everyone had the same burning passion as herself. Not that he had a burning passion, but he reckoned you needed some sort of commitment. No one endured an hour of torture like the one they'd just been through purely for the fun of it. He said as much to Steven, who hunched a shoulder.

'You could be right. It's just that I haven't made up my mind yet. It's a bit like deciding to go into a monastery — dedication, and all that crap. I don't mind the hard work, it's not that that bugs me, it's all the bullshit that goes with it. All the camp. The *bal*lay . . . as if it's some kind of sacred shrine.'

Yes, he'd had some of that from Anita. She tended to speak of 'The Ballet' as if it were an object of worship. He'd had a go at her about it once. Since then she'd striven to be a bit more rational (at least, in front of him: there was no telling what she was like all day with her mates at Kendra Hall) but every so often, even now, she'd have a relapse and go all glassy-eyed and reverential.

'Anyway,' said Steven, 'the whole business is lousy with flaming poufdahs. Look at that old Winston Woo . . . a right little raver. *And* the Lady Hamilton. Talk about flaunting herself! Next time round, if she's not careful, she'll come back as a peacock.'

'You mean peahen,' said Jamie.

It occurred to him, afterwards, that peahen was wrong, since peahens didn't have anything to flaunt, but it got a cheap laugh at the time.

He left Steven at the entrance to Ealing Common Underground and went on, up the road, to Auntie Margaret's. The house was called Wychwood, and although it wasn't as big as Kendra Hall, which had once been somebody or other's manor, still it was big enough. It was set back from the road, in a front garden the size of a park, with a vast sweeping driveway that went round in a semi-circle, and a flight of steps, enclosed in a sort of tunnel to keep out the rain, leading up to the front doors. The front doors were double, and opened on to more doors (also double) which in turn opened on to a huge square hall with other doors opening off, and in the middle a wide, curving staircase covered in red stair carpet going all the way up to the attics.

This evening, when he arrived back, he found Anita and Auntie Margaret watching television in one of the rooms on the left-hand side of the hall. (He had never known a house with so many rooms, they seemed to have a different one for everything they did, whether it was eating or watching television or just sitting down thinking.) Uncle Richard wasn't there, because he'd gone off on business. He was always going off on business. He was something important with Royal Dutch Shell and had, so Anita said vaguely, to attend 'conferences and things'. The Hunchback wasn't there, either, because he was safely tucked away back at university reading his history books, whilst the obnoxious Babs was at her boarding school in Surrey (telling all her little pals about bum bandits, he shouldn't wonder, and sifting through the Kama Sutra for things that sounded dirty).

He opened one of the double doors that led into the room where the television was kept and cautiously stuck his head round a couple of centimetres. You never knew when there was going to be company — one day last week he'd walked in on a whole dinner table full of them. In any case, the room was covered in white carpet which he was scared to tread on in his outdoor shoes. Usually he took them off and carried them, something which Auntie Margaret seemed to find amusing.

'Here comes Jamie,' she would say, 'carrying his shoes!'

He bet she wouldn't find it so amusing if he trod dog shit all over the place.

Tonight she said: 'Hallo, Jamie! Had a good day?'

Anita bounced round in her chair.

'Did you enjoy it?'

'Yeah; it was OK.'

'You look tired,' said Auntie Margaret.

'Did you have Mr Bregonzi? Don't you think he's super?'

'There's some of Mrs Archer's brown stew downstairs if you're hungry. It only needs heating up.'

He declined the stew in favour of bed: it had suddenly come upon him that he was not only tired but half dead on his feet. That hour with Attila the Hun, coming as it had at the end of a day humping crates with Charlie and Big Mac, had just about finished him.

'Take a bath if you want one,' said Auntie Margaret.

She was always urging him to take baths. So far, he hadn't been able to bring himself to do so, the reason being that the bathroom (one of the bathrooms: it seemed there were several) unnerved him. It didn't feel like a bathroom. It had a circular bath with brass shells instead of taps, and there was more of the white carpet on the floor. There was also a curious glass dome let into the ceiling, directly above the circular bath, which he didn't like the look of. It looked to him suspiciously like a spy hole. Today, being all of a muck sweat after the Hun, and not wanting aches and pains in the morning, he decided to take a chance and risk it. There was almost certainly a video camera concealed up there, but forewarned was forearmed: they needn't think they were getting *his* services free for their blue movies.

He washed himself, in a series of gymnastic contortions, in two seconds flat, decorously hopped into a bath towel, and hot-footed it down the passage to safety. Back in his bedroom, in his old pink pyjamas that had been bought three years ago for when he had had to go into hospital for his appendix, he did a few pliés, using the bedrail as a barre, just to reassure himself that he still could, and was on the point of climbing into bed when there was a tap at the door and Anita's voice said: 'Is it all right if I come in?' She was in anyway. He felt distinctly foolish, standing there in his old pink pyjamas. The jacket no longer buttoned across the chest and the legs came barely half way down his calves.

'What d'you want?' The words came out rather more ungraciously than he had intended, but it was embarrassing being seen by Anita in this state. Underpants he wouldn't have minded; but old pink *pyjamas* —

'I just wanted to know if you had Mr Bregonzi.'

'Yeah; we had him.'

'Did you like him? He's super, isn't he?'

'He's a sadist, if you ask me.' It wouldn't have been so bad if he'd had a dressing gown. At least

56

he could have hidden the worst of it.

'But did you *enjoy* it?'

'Yeah, I said . . . it was OK.'

'And you are going to go on with it?'

For crying out loud! He'd only just started.

''Course I'm going to go on with it.' Couldn't do much else in the circumstances, could he? He'd already burnt his boats. 'Look,' he said, 'I am a bit knackered —'

He didn't actually say, so if you wouldn't mind shoving off, I could get into bed and get my head down, but the message, obviously, got across. A spot of pink appeared in Anita's cheeks, as it had at Christmas when he'd given her her present.

'Sorry,' she said. 'I didn't realize.'

She walked, stiff-backed, from the room. Now he'd gone and upset her. He knew a moment's temptation to go after her and tell her that he hadn't meant to, but it just wasn't dignified; not in old pink pyjamas. Anyway, people oughtn't to come crashing in and out of other people's bedrooms. God knows, he'd told Kim about it often enough. You wouldn't think he'd have to tell Anita.

Grumpily, he crawled into bed, beneath the continental quilt. He didn't *enjoy* upsetting people — he didn't *enjoy* having to be curt. If only they would just use a bit of forethought; that was all it took. A simple bit of forethought and these little unpleasantnesses need never arise. Perhaps tomorrow evening he'd take her down the road for a coffee (a coffee being about as much as he could run to) then she could talk about the Hun to her heart's content. That would make her happy.

Duly, the following evening, he hurried straight back — only to find that Anita was not there. Auntie Margaret said she'd gone to the ballet with a friend from dancing school.

'A girl friend,' she added.

He didn't care if it *was* a girl friend (that was a lie: he did). He still felt put out. She might at least have told him. If he'd known she wasn't going to be there he'd have gone for a coffee with Steven. Steven had said to him, as they left Kendra Hall, 'Coming for a coffee?' and Jamie had thought of Anita and how he was going to say nice things to her, to make up for turfing her out of his room the previous night, and now he got back to find that she was out amusing herself. Well, she needn't think he was making the effort a second time. Tomorrow night, if Steven suggested they go for a coffee, he'd go for a coffee and be hanged to her.

The following night, needless to say, Steven didn't even mention the word coffee. Probably sick of Jamie making excuses. After a bit, diffidently, as they approached the Underground, Jamie said: 'Got time to stop off somewhere?' but now it was Steven who made the excuses.

''Fraid not, I've got to get back. Got a mate coming round.'

He didn't imagine for one moment that it was true.

'Tell you what,' said Steven. 'How about coming out for a drink Friday night?'

Jamie hesitated. They didn't have a class Friday

night; on the other hand he didn't fancy having to suffer the indignity, in front of Steven, of going into a pub and being told to get the hell out.

'Or, if you like, we could just go up the West End and mosey around for a bit. Call in for fish and chips — look at the loonies in Leicester Square. You ever been up there at night?' Jamie shook his head. 'In that case, my son, your education is sadly lacking. You come along with your Uncle Steven and let him broaden your outlook.'

'OK,' said Jamie. It was about time he had his eyes opened to some of the seamier things of life — the things they were always going on about in the Sunday papers. Sex shops, prostitutes. He probably wouldn't even recognize a prostitute if he saw one. Steven was right: his education *was* lacking.

When he arrived back at Auntie Margaret's, Anita was waiting for him. She seemed anxious.

'Jamie, I'm sorry I was out last night.'

Why, he wondered? Why was she sorry? She had every right to go out.

'It's just that we were given these free tickets ... we've got some more for Friday. I thought perhaps —' the colour was in her cheeks again — 'I thought perhaps you might like to come.'

Why did these things always have to happen to him?

'I would've,' he said, 'but I've just gone and arranged to do something else.'

'Oh. Oh, well, never mind. It was just an idea. I can always go with Belinda.'

'I would've come,' he said.

59

'It doesn't matter,' said Anita. 'I don't expect you'd have liked it very much. It's modern.'

Just as he had expected, he didn't recognize a prostitute when he saw one.

'That was one,' Steven kept saying. 'So was that, I bet you . . . and that over there, in the mock leopard skin. She's on the game, you can tell.'

He wondered how — they all looked like perfectly ordinary women to him.

'Don't worry,' said Steven, kindly. 'You'll learn. When you've been around as long as I have.'

Steven, in point of fact, had been around barely eighteen months longer than Jamie; he just seemed to have packed in a lot more experience. For a start, he had been thrown out of school (he volunteered the information quite happily) at the age of sixteen on account of what he called 'my attitude'.

'It was a boarding school — very stuffy establishment. They didn't like the way I looked at things. Said I gave the place a bad image.'

'I bet your folks were mad,' said Jamie.

'Not really. They just said I'd better get off my backside and start learning to shift for myself.'

Steven had been shifting for himself for the last couple of years. It taught you, he said, a thing or two.

'Like, basically, how to get what you want out of life . . . I've learnt you can always get what you want if you just set about it in the right way. Like I decided to go for these ba*lay* classes when I didn't have so much as a cent to my name. So what happens?'

Jamie shook his head.

'I get to do this movie, don't I?' said Steven, lapsing into the pseudo-American accent he affected from time to time. 'OK, so it's no big deal, it's not going to make me a star overnight, but what it does, it gives me enough bread to pay for the classes. Of course, now I've paid for them I have to decide whether they're really what I want. If they are, then I stick with them; if they're not —' He shrugged. 'I move on to the next thing. Whatever that next thing turns out to be. You can't tell till it happens. But that, in a nutshell, my son, is the Bothwell philosophy . . . just take life as it comes, and sod the lot of 'em.'

Jamie wondered if he could live like that; he didn't think that he could. He liked to be able to see some sort of path ahead of him — some sort of goal waiting to be reached. There didn't seem to him to be much point in life if you didn't have something to aim at.

'I do have something to aim at,' said Steven. 'I aim at having fun. What else is there?'

On Saturday morning they had an hour's class with Ben Bregonzi, followed by a half-hour break, followed by a pas de deux class, again with Ben Bregonzi, but with the welcome addition, this time, of eight assorted females.

Correction: nine. Another had just walked in. Jamie felt his throat go dry. Surely with all this lot at his disposal he ought to be able to make it with at least *one*?

'So which d'you fancy?' muttered Steven.

He swallowed. He rather fancied the one who had just walked in. She was small and dark, with curly black hair, cut very short, unlike most dancers', and she had this little elfin face, demure but sort of cheeky at the same time. Steven followed the direction of his gaze.

'Mm . . . not bad. Not bad at all. Of course, you won't get to partner her, you realize that? She'll get stuck with old Winston. Only one who's short enough for him — there! What did I tell you? Some waste . . .'

For most of the class Jamie was put to work with a girl called Doreen, who was thin and foxy-looking, with slightly buck teeth and reddish hair. He'd never really gone for girls with red hair. Mentally he set Doreen aside as a last resort. The little dark one — Pauline, her name was — was definitely top of the list. After her, there was a girl called Kate whom he wouldn't mind getting his end away with. She was rather round and bubbly, and she had a giggle, but there was something about her that did things to him. He put her down as number two. Number three he couldn't quite decide on. It was either a black girl called Bettina — except that Errol was already making it pretty plain he intended to lay claim to her — or if not Bettina, then maybe the blonde bombshell at present dissipating her energies trying to attract the Lady Hamilton (who was still wearing her vomit-green tights and scarlet leg warmers). He didn't know the blonde's name, but she didn't look like the sort of girl who would say no in a hurry. That was the only reason he hesitated over her. Girls who didn't say no tended to be girls who'd crammed in a lot of experience, like old Marigold Johnson, back at Tenterden, who according to Doug would practically rape you. Not that he wanted to have to *fight* anyone for it — and in any case, this one could hardly be compared with Marigold Johnson. Marigold had been short and squat and rather spotty: this one was tall and willowy and looked like a Scandinavian sex goddess. He reckoned he could stand being raped by a sex goddess. She might as well go down as number three.

As he stood watching Ben Bregonzi punch Graham into some sort of shape (Graham tended to flow about a bit, like a half-set jelly) he ran through his list in his mind:

No. 1 Small dark Pauline
No. 2 Round bubbly Kate
No. 3 Big blonde sex goddess
Reserve: Foxy Doreen.

If he couldn't make it with *one* of them before the year was out, then he might as well give up trying.

The following Saturday (he was still attempting, without success, to nerve himself to approach Pauline) Steven said: 'You still interested in getting a place of your own?'

'You bet!'

He was even more interested now than he had

been before. After all, if he were going to start making it with birds — which he most certainly *was*, sooner or later — he was going to need somewhere where he could take them. He couldn't very well smuggle them up to his bedroom at Auntie Margaret's.

'I had a word with my landlord,' said Steven. 'He says he's got this double bed-sit coming vacant in one of his other houses — just round the corner from where I am now. If we want it we can have it. I said I'd let him know first thing Monday — in case you wanted to check with your folks.'

'Yeah.' He supposed he ought at least to mention it to them. Not that he could see any likelihood of their objecting — after all, what was there to object to? He was the one who'd be paying for it, out of the money he earned at Plumber's.

'It's twenty-five quid a week,' said Steven. 'That OK?'

'Sure.'

It wouldn't leave him a great deal to live on — in fact, it would leave him hardly anything at all — but he reckoned it would be worth it, just to have a place of his own. He felt a bit like a farmyard animal, at Auntie Margaret's. He'd have been happier living down in the kitchen than clumping about upstairs amongst the glass-topped coffee tables, in perpetual fear of breakages or trekking dirt across the carpet. It wasn't even as if he saw anything of Anita. When he left in the mornings, for an eight-thirty start at Plumber's, she wasn't yet up: when he arrived at

64

Kendra Hall in the evening, for a meal in the canteen, she had already left; and by the time he got back at night, after a day spent lugging crates and an hour and a bit of the Hun, he felt fit for nothing but a hot-water soak beneath the spy hole (he was growing used to it by now: he even, on occasion, made rude gestures at it, just to show his contempt) and a quick dash back along the passage in his pink pyjamas to bed. The only times he ever really saw Anita were on Saturday mornings, at breakfast, and again on Sunday evening, when Daddy drove them both back to Ealing in the XJS. If he had a place of his own he wouldn't need to keep bumming lifts back, because he wouldn't need to keep running home every weekend. He could stay up in town, with Steven, and broaden his outlook.

Casually, that evening, down in the off-licence, during a break in the Saturday night stream of booze-buyers, when his father was watching the old black-and-white television in the cubby hole at the back of the shop, and his mother was sitting knitting behind the counter, he said: 'I've decided to move into a room with someone, by the way.'

'Move into a room? What do you mean, move into a room?' His mother sounded aggrieved. 'You've already got a room, with Anita's aunt.'

'Yeah, well, I've decided to move out and go and share with someone else.'

'Which someone else?'

'Boy at dancing school. He's got this bed-sitter in Hammersmith. Wants me to go in with him. I said I'd check with you it was OK.'

'Well, I'm not sure that it is.' Mrs Carr put down her knitting and frowned. 'What do you want to go into a bed-sitting room for? What's the matter with where you are?'

'Nothing. Just don't feel comfortable.'

'Why don't you feel comfortable? I thought you had everything you could possibly want . . . I thought you said Anita's aunt was very pleasant.'

'Yeah, she is. But it's not the same as having a place of your own.'

'You're not old enough to have a place of your own. I should worry all the time what you were getting up to.'

'There's nothing I *can* get up to. I'm working all day, I've got classes every night —'

'You wouldn't eat properly.'

'I would eat properly!'

'Hm!'

'Honestly, it wouldn't make an atom of difference.'

'I don't know.' Mrs Carr pursed her lips. 'On your own like that . . . you could get into all sorts of trouble.'

'I wouldn't *be* on my own. I'd be with someone else.'

'Yes, some boy as irresponsible as you are! How old is he?'

'Nineteen,' said Jamie, stretching a point.

'Nineteen. Well, there you are.' Mrs Carr picked up her knitting, as if to signify that as far as she was concerned the matter had now been settled. 'He'd lead you astray. I know what you're like, you're easily influenced. I'm not having you get yourself into trouble.'

'What sort of trouble?'

'Girls,' said Mrs Carr. She knitted, vigorously. 'There'd be orgies and I don't know what.'

'There wouldn't be orgies!' What did she think he was? Some kind of super stud? If he could make it with just *one* girl he'd count himself lucky. 'It's only a bed-sit in Hammersmith, not a flaming penthouse!'

'I don't care what it is. I wouldn't be happy.'

'Well, I'm not happy where I am now.'

Mrs Carr said nothing; just pursed her lips even tighter and went on knitting. He watched her, in silent irritation. Slip one, slop one, drop two together. Didn't she *care* that he wasn't happy?

'Doesn't it bother you?' he said.

Mrs Carr said nothing.

'Doesn't it bother you at *all*?'

'Doesn't what bother me at all?'

'The fact that I'm not happy.'

'Why aren't you happy? You're doing what you wanted, you're going to dancing school. What more do you want?'

'I want a place of my own.'

Mrs Carr made a row of rapid holes in her knitting.

'I don't see what the problem is . . . just moving into a bed-sitting room. If other people can do it, I don't see why I can't. It's not as if I'm an idiot. It's not as if I'm an imbecile. And anyway, I'll be seventeen next month.'

He thought for a moment that she wasn't

67

going to respond; but then, with an air of martyr-dom, she said: 'I've said all I have to say. You'd better ask your father.'

He knew, then, that the battle was as good as won. When she said 'You'd better ask your father' it meant that he'd managed to talk her round but that she just didn't want to admit it. He waited till she was serving a customer, then went through to the cubby hole behind the shop to tackle Mr Carr.

'Mum says it's OK by her if it's OK by you.'

'So long as you can afford it,' said Mr Carr. 'I'm pushed to the limit as it is, paying for those classes. I can't fork out for anything else.'

'I can afford it,' said Jamie.

'You reckon? Well, I don't suppose it'll do you any harm. You're a sensible lad, I'm sure you can be trusted not to get up to anything I wouldn't.'

'Absolutely,' said Jamie.

He went back out again to the shop.

'Dad hasn't any objections,' he said.

Mrs Carr sighed.

'No, he wouldn't have . . . no imagination, your father.'

Jamie wasn't sure about that. He reckoned his dad had imagination all right.

'Can I go and ring Steven, then?' he said. 'Tell him it's on?'

'I suppose so,' said Mrs Carr. She picked up her knitting again from beneath the counter. He wondered what it was supposed to be — it looked like some kind of a shroud. The holes, pre-sumably, were part of the pattern. 'This is for you,' said Mrs Carr. She held it out for his approval. 'I thought you could do with another sweater.'

He swallowed.

'Yeah,' he said. 'Great.'

At least if he were living away from home he wouldn't actually have to be seen wearing the thing; that was some consolation.

4

'Look, if you fancy it,' said Steven, 'then go and ask it.'

'Yeah —'

There was a pause.

'Well, go on, then!' Steven gave a little push, by way of encouragement. 'Don't just sit there . . . go on over and do it!'

Jamie scraped his chair back, still uncertain. He looked across the canteen at Pauline, little and dark, with her cheeky elfin face. He *did* fancy her, but it wasn't that easy. At school, you just went up to a girl — like it might be Sharon, or her friend with the funny name, Coral Flaskett — and said 'Feel like coming down the disco Saturday night? Feel like coming to the Jazz Club?' and the girl either said yes, or she said no, and that was that; simple. Living in a bed-sit in Hammersmith, paying £25 a week rent and earning a pittance at Plumber's, meant that he couldn't afford to go casually inviting girls out to discos and jazz clubs just whenever he felt like it. He'd acquired a place of his own to take people back to, but you couldn't very well take them back unless you'd taken them out somewhere in the first place.

'I dunno,' he said. 'I dunno where I could take her.'

'You can't mean it! After all the pains I've been at to improve your education? All those naughty night clubs I've shown you? All those wicked flesh pots I've introduced you to? And you say, you don't know where to take her?'

'I know plenty of places I *could* take her . . . it's a question of having the money to take her with.'

'Ah! What you mean is, you have a cash flow problem? That begins to make sense — that I can understand and appreciate.'

'It kind of cuts down one's options.'

'It does indeed, my son.'

'I suppose I could always just take her up the road for a burger —'

'Tacky,' said Steven. 'Decidedly tacky.'

'All right, then! You suggest something.'

'How about a party?'

'Don't know any parties.'

'I do,' said Steven. 'Girl friend of mine's giving one. This Saturday. Why not bring her along to that, then at a suitable stage in the evening you can twinkle her back home and I'll guarantee to stay out of the way until the small hours. How about that for a brilliant idea?'

'Where is it?' said Jamie. 'This party?'

'Edgware Road — no problem. Straight through on the Metropolitan.'

'OK.' With fresh determination, he thrust back his chair. 'I'll ask her.'

He caught Pauline as she was paying for her meal at the cash desk. Foxy Doreen had just walked past, bearing a tray full of shepherd's pie and chips. Pauline, he was pleased to note, had more aesthetic tastes: like Anita, she stuck to green salads and yoghourt. He handed her some cutlery, from the plastic cutlery box. She seemed surprised.

'What's this for?'

'For you — to eat with.'

'Oh.' She took them from him and placed them on her tray. She still seemed surprised. 'Did you want something?'

'Wanted to ask if you'd like to come to a party with me on Saturday.'

'A party?' She considered the idea, head to one side. 'Whereabouts?'

'Edgware Road.'

'Edgware Road?'

He wondered if she was going to repeat absolutely everything that he said.

'Yes,' he said. 'Edgware Road.'

He waited for her to say it again, but she merely wrinkled her nose and looked doubtful.

'There's no problem,' he said. 'It's straight through on the Metropolitan.'

'But I don't live on the Metropolitan.'

'Ah —' That was something that hadn't occurred to him. 'So where do you live?'

'I live out at Wimbledon, and that's on the District.'

District: that was the green one. He tried to see it on the tube map.

'Well, that's all right,' he said. 'You can get the tube up to Hammersmith and I'll meet you there.'

'Earl's Court,' she said.

'OK. Earl's Court.'

'I'd have to change, to get to Hammersmith.'

'Yeah, OK. Earl's Court's OK by me.'

'And you'll take me home afterwards?'

''Course I'll take you home afterwards.' After she'd been back to Hammersmith. He'd do anything she wanted, after she'd been back to Hammersmith.

'I have to be in by midnight. My parents are very strict.'

'No sweat.' He calculated rapidly. Suppose they got to the party for, say, nine, left again at ten, got back to Hammersmith by ten-thirty — that was cutting it a bit fine. They'd have to get to the party for eight, then they could leave again at nine-fifteen — well, say nine-thirty; that would give them an hour and a half at the party, back to Hammersmith by ten, say they had to allow forty minutes for getting her home —

'Do you think we should move?' said Pauline. 'We're holding up the queue.'

Obligingly, he stepped back a pace.

'Want me to carry your tray for you?'

'That's all right, thank you. I can manage.'

'We've got a table over there, if you'd like to join us.'

'I can't,' she said. 'I'm with Doreen.'

'Ah. Well —' He stepped back another pace. 'I'll see you on Saturday, then. About seven-thirty?'

73

She looked at him, gravely.

'I should hope I'd be seeing you in class before then.'

'Oh — sure! I just wanted to make certain it was a definite date.'

'Yes,' said Pauline.

'Good. Great. Well —' Still walking backwards, he bumped into the corner of a table: it happened to be Doreen's. She regarded him, frostily.

'Do you mind?'

'Sorry,' he said. 'Wasn't looking where I was going.'

'I could see *that*,' said Doreen.

He sometimes thought that Doreen didn't like him very much — she had this tendency to be sharp. Still, whether she liked him or not hardly mattered any more: she was only down as reserve. If things went as they should with Pauline, he wouldn't have any need of her.

He made his way back to his own table.

'Looks good?' said Steven.

Jamie grinned.

'Looks good . . .'

There was only one point which still bothered him. If he *could* entice her back — and if, once she *was* back, she proved willing — what bothered him (assuming she actually *let* him) was whether it was up to *him*, or whether he could safely leave it to *her* —

'Leave what to her?' Steven seemed bewildered.

'Well — you know . . . precautions.'

Down in the men's lavatory, in the disco where

74

he and Doug used to go, they'd had one of these slot machines which for a small sum dispensed packets of Durex. Doug had always scorned it. 'Don't want to go bothering with crap like that. Not these days.' Doug had said that these days all women were on the Pill, and if they weren't then it was their own stupid fault. The only trouble was, he had grown out of of placing much reliance on Doug. Half the time, he had discovered, Doug didn't know any more than Jamie did.

'What you're talking about,' said Steven, 'is the mechanics. And that, my son, is the least of your problems. First get your girl; that's the difficult part.'

'Yeah. Well, assuming,' said Jamie, 'that I've got one —'

'You leave it to me.' Steven winked. 'I'll see you all right.'

That same evening, in the canteen before class, he slipped a small packet into Jamie's hand.

'What's this?' said Jamie.

'Compliments of the house . . . what is commonly known, my son, as a packet of three. To be kept always about your person for when the need should arise — well, don't go flashing it about in public, you steaming great nit!'

Guiltily, Jamie stowed it away in the back pocket of his jeans.

'Where'd you get it?'

'Out the shop. One of the little perks I was talking of.'

He was puzzled.

'I thought you said you worked in a bookshop?'

'A sort of bookshop . . . what you might call, highly specialized.'

'You mean —'

Steven tapped the side of his nose.

'Them as asks no questions gets told no lies . . . you just take what's offered and keep stumm.'

On Saturday evening, when he and Steven arrived at Earl's Court, Pauline was already there, waiting. She was dressed all in black, with neat little suede boots and a coat with a big furry collar. Fortunately he'd had a hunch she might be the dressy type and taken the precaution of putting on a tie and his one and only jacket.

'Sorry if we're late,' said Steven. 'It was his fault, he couldn't decide which tie to wear, his or mine . . . we've got all of two between us, so you can see it was a big decision.'

'That's all right,' said Pauline. 'You're not late, I was early. I'm always early, wherever I go. It's a sort of obsession.'

'And a very good one, I'm sure,' said Steven.

'I don't know.' She screwed up her nose, making her face look more elfin than ever. 'I once read that people who are always early are basically very insecure.'

'And is that what you are?'

'Oh, yes; terribly.'

Steven raised an eyebrow.

'I can't imagine,' he murmured, 'what you have to be insecure about . . .'

It was Jamie, at that moment, who was feeling

insecure. He didn't care for the way that Steven was taking over — almost as if he were the one who had asked her out. They caught the tube to Edgware Road, and Pauline sat between them, but it was Steven whom she talked to rather than Jamie. Probably that was because Jamie couldn't think of anything very much to say, whereas Steven had a never-ending flow of banter which obviously amused. He couldn't hear more than the odd snatches above the rattle of the train, but he knew that it amused because Steven's banter always did, and in any case Pauline kept laughing and screwing up her nose.

'Steven's funny, isn't he?' she said, when at last they had reached the party and were alone together (Steven, who was apparently familiar with the place, having gone off in search of someone called Emilia).

'Yes,' said Jamie. 'I suppose he is.'

'I like people who are funny.'

'Actually,' said Jamie, 'he does already have a girl friend.'

'Oh! I wouldn't want to go *out* with him,' said Pauline.

He wanted to ask her why not, but at that moment Steven appeared with the girl called Emilia and he didn't have a chance. He kept wondering about it all night.

The party, he guessed, was pretty reasonable — he didn't have much to compare it with. People at Tenterden, on the whole, hadn't gone in for parties, they'd mostly congregated in the clubs or disco. He would have enjoyed himself more if he'd felt a bit less juvenile, but at least Pauline stuck with him and didn't show any inclination to go waltzing off with any of the more mature types that were draped about the place. He was glad about that, because there certainly wasn't any other female there whom he fancied, they were all way out of his age range. He'd been trying to decide which one was Steven's girl friend, whether it was Sue, who was giving the party, or Emilia, who had a room in Sue's flat. Sue was tall, and a bit mannish, striding round in black pants and cowboy boots: Emilia was short and rather stubby, with curly hair and a freckled face. Sue was the better looking, but Emilia seemed nicer natured. They were both of them somewhat on the old side — mid-twenties, he would have said, although he wasn't very good at assessing women's ages. He tried asking Pauline, but Pauline only sniffed and said scornfully, 'About fifty, I should think.' He put that down to simple female jealousy, on account of one of them being Steven's girl friend. (He settled at last for Sue, as being the more sophisticated, though as Steven divided his time pretty well equally between the two it was hard to be certain.)

At half past nine, he suggested to Pauline that perhaps they should be going now.

'Oh, not yet!' she cried. 'We've only just come!'

'Actually, we've been here an hour and a half,' said Jamie.

'Well, what's an hour and a half? We're at a party!'

'Yeah, but you said you'd got to get home —'

'By *mid*night,' said Pauline.

He gave her another fifteen minutes, then tried again:

'Did you know that it's quarter to ten?'

'Gosh!' said Pauline. She opened her eyes very wide, in the way that Kim had recently taken to doing. Kim's eyes were like little boot buttons: Pauline's were large and lamp-like. 'Gosh!' she said again. 'Is it really?'

He was almost taken in.

'Well, I thought I'd better tell you . . . seeing as you have this obsession about always being early.'

'Only when I'm going to places — not when I'm leaving them.'

'But if we went now,' he said, 'we could have a coffee. *And* something to eat.'

In his experience (admittedly limited) girls could never resist the lure of something to eat. He'd taken the precaution of laying in a stock of baked beans and some tins of chipolatas.

'Oh, all right,' said Pauline. 'I suppose we might as well . . . it's not much of a party, anyhow. They're all so ancient.'

Good, thought Jamie; that meant they still had time to make it back to Hammersmith. He felt in his jacket pocket to check that the packet of three was still in there: it was. That was all right. First get your girl . . .

'Look,' said Pauline, as they emerged into the Edgware Road. She pointed. 'There's an Egg and Spoon. We could go in there.'

'We don't want to go in there.' He placed a

hand beneath her elbow, carefully steering her in the opposite direction, towards the Underground. 'Let's go back to my place.'

'But I'd rather go to the Egg and Spoon.'

'No, you wouldn't,' he said. 'They're horrible. They're disgusting. They don't clean the tables properly. You come back to my place.'

'But I don't want to come back to your place.'

'Why not? It's nice at my place.' They were veering off course again, towards the Egg and Spoon. Firmly, he re-directed them. 'It'll only take five minutes.'

'What will?'

'Getting there.'

'It'll only take five seconds, getting to the Egg and Spoon.'

'Yeah, but I told you . . . my place is nicer than the Egg and Spoon.'

'I don't see how it can be. You've only got a bed-sitter.'

'I know, but it's a very nice bed-sitter.'

'Well, I'm not coming there,' said Pauline.

'But I've got food in,' he said.

'I can't help that, I'm still not coming. If you wanted a girl who'd do that sort of thing, you should have asked Natalie. She'd do it with any-one. And if you want to give me something to eat' — he wasn't sure that he did, any more — 'you can give it to me here.'

Somehow or other, she had managed to turn him round, so that they were standing directly outside the Egg and Spoon. He had no alter-native but to go in.

'I'll have egg, sausages and chips,' said Pauline. (So much for the green salads and yoghourt.) 'How about you?'

Rapidly totting up the amount of money in his pocket — bearing in mind he still had to get her all the way out to Wimbledon — he said: 'I'm not hungry. I'll just have a coffee.'

He watched glumly as the waitress took down the order and went to shout it through to the kitchen.

'I expect you think I'm very peculiar,' said Pauline.

He shrugged. He had given up thinking women peculiar: they were just raving potty, the whole lot of them. What with Anita, who thought of nothing but the ballet, and now this one, wittering on about being peculiar —

'I *know* you think I'm peculiar,' she said.

'All right, then.' If that was what she wanted — who was he to contradict her? 'So I think you're peculiar.'

'I knew you did.' Now she was happy. 'Men always do, but I can't help it . . . it's part of my insecurity thing.'

'What is?'

'The fact that I don't want to go back with them to have sex.'

Maybe she should have gone into a nunnery. Maybe they should all go into nunneries. It would be better than walking round inciting people — and anyway, no one had asked her to come back and have sex.

'All I was suggesting,' he said, 'was a coffee.'

She looked at him, reproachfully. He could almost feel her eyes boring their way into his jacket pocket.

'So what's with all this insecurity thing?' he said.

That was better; that was what she wanted. She wanted to talk about herself and tell him why she didn't want to have sex. She leaned forward, across the table.

'Once when I was young,' she said, 'when I was about eleven, I saw this naked man.'

'Oh, yes?'

'It was dreadful.'

There was a pause. He waited for her to say what was dreadful about it.

'I mean, there he was,' said Pauline, 'lying in this field . . . *naked. Doing* things.'

'Gosh,' said Jamie, getting his own back.

'You can say gosh,' said Pauline, 'but it wasn't a very nice sight, I can tell you. As a matter of fact, it was pretty revolting.'

'Men are pretty revolting,' said Jamie. 'I don't know why you come out with us at all.'

'I wouldn't go out with just anybody,' said Pauline. 'I wouldn't go out with Errol, for example.'

'Why not?' He bristled, prepared to leap to the defence. 'What's wrong with Errol?'

'He's very sexual,' said Pauline.

'Is he?' He'd never noticed Errol being very sexual; but then, perhaps, he wouldn't. Perhaps he was only sexual when there were women around. 'What about Steven?' he said. 'Why wouldn't you go out with him?'

'I never go out with older men. They're not easy to control.'

Did that mean that he *was* easy to control? He glowered at her, as the coffee arrived. Why was it he could never learn to be masterful? He bet if he were Steven he'd have her back in Hammersmith by now — not only back in Hammersmith, but actually in *bed*.

'D'you know who the nicest boy is?' said Pauline. 'The nicest one of all? It's Percy. He's sweet; he really is. I wouldn't mind going out with Percy. I'd feel safe with Percy. I wouldn't feel safe with Brett.'

'Really?' said Jamie. This was growing interesting. The female psychology never failed to surprise. 'Why wouldn't you feel safe with Brett? He's not likely to do you any harm.'

'That's where you're so wrong,' said Pauline. 'Just because he's a bit camp it doesn't mean to say that he's what you think he is.'

Fascinating.

'What about Graham?' he said.

'Oh, I wouldn't go out with Graham,' said Pauline. 'I don't fancy *him*.'

He wondered what she meant by fancying someone. Obviously not what he meant.

The egg, sausages and chips had now put in an appearance, along with the attendant roll and butter. He watched for a while as she tucked into it. For all she was so tiny and delicate-looking, she was going at it like a garbage gobbler. It was a phenomenon he'd noticed before: it was always the little shrimp-like ones that stuffed themselves. Anita never did. Anita's appetite was quite normal and healthy, she didn't have anorexia or anything, but he couldn't imagine her mopping up platefuls of egg and chips. If she'd been here, she'd probably just have had a coffee.

'I don't know whether I ought to feel flattered or insulted,' he said.

'What about?'

'You, deigning to come out with me.' He didn't know whether it was because she fancied him (whatever that might mean) or whether it was because she held him in contempt.

Pauline speared three chips together and neatly cut them in half. She was very dainty, in spite of gobbling.

'I only ever go out with people I like the look of,' she said.

That was all very well, but there was a flaw in it, wasn't there? *She* liked the look of Percy.

'Also,' said Pauline, 'I knew you weren't the sort to care only about One Thing. You can always tell the ones that do . . . they have a funny look about them.' She placed her knife and fork precisely together on her empty plate. 'Shall we go now?'

On the way to Wimbledon (Paddington, Bayswater, Notting Hill Gate: High Street Kensington, Earl's Court, *change*. West Brompton, Fulham Broadway: Parson's Green, Putney Bridge: East Putney, Southfields, Wimbledon Park, *Wimbledon*) she told him more

84

about the naked man, the sight of whom had been so dreadful. It was evidently a subject which engrossed her.

'I mean, can you *imagine*?' she said. 'When I was only *eleven*?'

He thought of Babs, who was also only eleven. He bet if she saw a naked man she wouldn't turn a hair. What, after all, was a naked man to one who had read *Lady Chatterley*? The chances were she'd go running over to take a closer look.

'It's not very *big*, is it? My brother's is *loads* bigger than that.'

At least she wouldn't end up with a complex. (If anyone did, it would be the naked man.) He began slightly to revise his ideas on the subject of sex education: perhaps there was something to be said, after all, for reading *Lady Chatterley* at the age of eleven.

Dutifully, he accompanied Pauline to her front door. She lived in a street all full of semi-detacheds (nothing grand, like Anita's, but still a cut above the flat over the off-licence) in a house called Vinrosa, which at first he thought must be *vin rosé* in Italian, but Pauline said no, it was short for Vincent and Rosemary. He was tempted even now to try kissing her, but he supposed he'd better not. Not with her hang-ups. She'd probably start screaming the place down, and he didn't relish the idea of some angry parent rushing out with a pickaxe, or being had up on a charge of indecent assault. Apart from anything else, it might get into the papers and then his mother would die of shame, and Anita would never speak to him again. (Or would she? It was hard to be certain, with Anita. She had only one set of morals, and they were centred entirely on the ballet: *being able to dance is the only thing that matters . . .*)

'Thank you for inviting me,' said Pauline. 'I really enjoyed it. It's really good, being with someone who doesn't think only of One Thing.'

He thought exclusively of only One Thing all the way back from Wimbledon (change at Earl's Court) to Hammersmith. He had to wait almost twenty minutes for a train from Wimbledon, and another fifteen for a connection at Earl's Court, and thoughts of One Thing preoccupied him to such an extent that at Earl's Court he very nearly took a train going east instead of west, which would have landed him up heaven knows where, Dagenham or Upminster or some such place.

When finally he arrived back, Steven was there. (He could have wished that he wasn't.)

'I left it as long as I could,' said Steven, 'but the party kind of disintegrated. How did you make out?'

'Oh —' He shrugged. 'OK.'

'You don't sound over-enthusiastic?'

'No, well, she has this thing . . . saw some guy whacking off in a field at the age of eleven. Never got over it.'

'A likely tale!' Steven laughed. 'Whacking off in a field . . . she's putting you on!'

Was she? — could she be? For just a moment, he had doubts.

'Well, anyway,' he said, 'it's no use you trying

your luck, she doesn't go out with older men. She
told me so.'

'Get her!' jeered Steven.

Jamie couldn't be sure whether he was referring
to Pauline or to himself. Disgruntled, he climbed
into his pink pyjamas and into bed.

'I'm going to turn the light out,' he said. He did
so. 'All right?'

He waited for Steven, as a matter of principle,
to say no; instead, through the darkness, came a
chuckle.

'Sweet dreams . . . or should I say wet ones?'

'Get knotted!' Jamie pulled the covers up over
his head. There were times when life could be very
trying; very trying indeed.

5

What with the fares to Earl's Court, and the fares
to the Edgware Road, not to mention the fares all
the way to and from Wimbledon (one of them
double) plus a couple of coffees and a plateful of
egg, sausages and chips, *plus* a roll and butter,
plus a bottle of cider to take to the party, he had
just about blown himself out. By the middle of
the week, with his next pay packet still only a
faint dot on the horizon, ten days away, he was
having to borrow from Steven and live off his
stock of baked beans and chipolatas. It came as
almost a relief when Anita rang him up to ask if
he were interested in having a lift home in
Daddy's XJS on Saturday afternoon. He had, as
a matter of fact, made a vow not to go home for at
least a month, to demonstrate his independence
and ability to cope; but since she was *offering* —

'Where shall I see you?' he said.

'Auntie Margaret's? Two o'clock?'

'I'll be there,' said Jamie.

Auntie Margaret had been surprisingly
sympathetic about his moving out. He'd been a
bit worried, to tell the truth, in case she might

take it personally, but all she'd said was, 'Jamie, my dear boy, you don't have to apologize. Believe it or not, I *can* still remember what it was like to be young. You want a place of your own: I perfectly understand.' It had been Anita who hadn't understood.

'But *why*?' she'd kept saying. 'I don't see the point.'

She still didn't, because how could he explain? 'I want a place where I can take girls back . . .' Auntie Margaret obviously understood, and obviously Daddy did, too.

'So! You've set up an independent establishment, have you?' He turned, and gave Jamie a wink, as he swung the XJS out of Auntie Margaret's driveway. 'Got yourself a flat, eh?'

'Actually, it's a bed-sitting room,' said Anita.

'Well, that's still a sight better than a poke in the eye with a burnt stick . . . nothing like having a place of your own.'

'It's not his own,' said Anita. 'He shares.'

'Ah, yes!' said Daddy. 'But there's a world of difference between sharing with someone your own age and sharing with some crusty old fuddy duddy of a geriatric, isn't there, Jamie?'

'It does mean you can do things,' agreed Jamie.

'I'm sure it does!'

There was a pause, while Daddy manoeuvred the car into the stream of Saturday afternoon traffic.

'What sort of things?' said Anita.

Daddy, at that, threw back his head and roared. Jamie resisted the temptation to join in:

the pinkness had come into Anita's cheeks and he
didn't like to see her embarrassed.

'It means you can go out and leave things,' he
said, 'instead of having to keep putting them
away all the time. Like if the bed's not made, or
the sink's full of stuff, there's nobody to nag at
you.'

'God!' said Daddy. 'Shades of the past . . . I'll
bet the place is a shambles!'

'It's not exactly spotless,' admitted Jamie.

'I'll bet it isn't! Needs a woman's hand, by the
sound of things.' Daddy shot an amused glance
at Anita. 'Wouldn't you say?'

'I wouldn't know,' said Anita. 'I've never been
asked round there.'

She turned, and looked out of the window.
Jamie stared at her, in anguish. *He* hadn't known
she wanted to be asked round — he'd thought
she wasn't interested. That was the impression
she'd given, the day he'd moved out. It had been
Auntie Margaret who'd wanted to know everything, like whether they were on the telephone,
and whether there were cooking facilities. Anita
had seemed not to care.

He worried about it all weekend — about
Anita wanting to be asked round, and him not
asking her. He didn't like to telephone her and
make a special point of it; it would be too obvious.
On the other hand, he didn't want to do it in front
of Daddy, on the way back. This was something
between him and Anita. In the end, he managed
to get her by herself for just five minutes while
Daddy was backing the car out of the garage.

'You doing anything Friday?' he said.

'No,' said Anita. 'I don't think so. Why?'

'I was wondering if you'd like to come round to our place.'

Now she'd gone all pink again. He'd never known her keep going pink like this before. Perhaps it was just something that happened to girls at her age.

'All right,' she said.

'Come round for a coffee. About eight o'clock.'

'All right.'

Eight o'clock would give him time to get back from Plumber's and stuff some baked beans down himself. Give him a chance to do a bit of tidying up, as well. He wouldn't like Anita to see the place as it was. He wondered whether Steven was going to be in, or whether (hopefully) he'd be going round to Sue's place. He'd asked him, the day after the party, which one it was who was his girl friend, Sue or Emilia. Steven had laughed and said, 'Turn and turn about . . . depends which one I happen to fancy at the time.'

It would be rather nice, thought Jamie, if he could be persuaded into fancying one or other of them on Friday night. Tentatively, he suggested the idea.

'Why?' said Steven, at once. 'What dirty little plots are you hatching now?'

'Nothing. I've asked Anita round, that's all.'

'So why do you want me out of the way? I thought you didn't have anything going between you?'

'Well . . . no; not in that sense.' Unfortunately.

'So why can't I just look in and say hallo?'

'S'pose you can if you really want.'

'I do want; I'm interested. I want to see what's so special about her.'

'There isn't anything special about her. She's just someone I happen to know.'

'Oh? You could have fooled me,' said Steven.

The remark bothered him. What did he mean by it? *You could have fooled me.* What was that supposed to imply?

'Well,' said Steven, 'she obviously wields great influence over you ... Anita says this, Anita says that ... Anita does such and such, Anita thinks so and so ... I not unnaturally concluded that she must be of some importance in your life.'

She was of importance; of course she was. If it hadn't been for Anita, he might even now be signing on as unemployed or still kicking his heels at Tenterden. On the other hand, he resented the suggestion that she wielded any influence over him. He wasn't as easily influenced as some people seemed to think.

To prove the point, he didn't bother tidying up on Friday night. *He* liked the place the way it was, so Anita would just have to put up with it. It might not be what she was used to, but so what? Not everyone wanted to live with white carpets and glass-topped coffee tables. He half expected her to take one look and say '*Jamie*, it's a *midden*,' but in fact she seemed quite struck with it.

'It's nice,' she said. 'You are lucky ... I wish I had a place like this.'

He was gratified.

'Like me to try and find one for you?'

Regretfully, she shook her head.

'Wouldn't do any good if you did. They won't let me — not till September. I'll be eighteen in September. They've promised me I can then, if I want.'

He kept forgetting that she was five months older than he was. In many ways, it sometimes seemed to him, Anita's education was even more lacking than his own. For all she was used to dining in posh restaurants and going shopping with Mummy in Harrod's, and spending her holidays abroad, when it came to the ordinary, basic things of life her ignorance never ceased to astound. He'd asked her, at Christmas, whether she was going to sign on for the vacation period, and she'd looked at him blankly and said: 'Sign on? Sign on where?' She didn't even know about signing on. If she were to be dumped in the middle of Piccadilly Circus without any money, she wouldn't have the least idea how to set about looking after herself.

'Take a seat,' he said.

He waved her towards the room's only armchair, but instead she chose to kneel on the hearth rug, in front of the gas fire. She was wearing a thick-knit sweater with a big floppy neck and a pair of stretch jeans tucked into boots. Her hair, as usual, was pulled back into an elastic band.

He made her some instant coffee and handed her a cup.

'I'd have done you some food or something,

except that I'm not a very good cook.'

'Neither am I,' said Anita. 'The domestic science mistress at school couldn't stand me. She said I must have hands like cement mixers. I don't know what I shall do if I move into a flat.'

'Live off baked beans,' he said. 'I do.'

He sat on the edge of the bed, cradling the mug of hot coffee between his knees. A silence fell. He sought for some way to break it.

'Have you —'

'Are you —'

They both spoke at the same time; both stopped.

'After you,' said Jamie.

'I was just going to say, are you still enjoying it . . . being at dancing school?'

'Yeah; it's great.'

'I knew you'd like it, once you were there.'

There was a pause.

'What were you —'

'I was just —'

'Go on,' said Anita.

'I was just going to ask how you were getting on?'

'Oh! Fine,' said Anita. 'We've got Miss Flowerdew this term, she's super. Much better than Miss Gover . . . ghastly Gover. She's really sarcastic.'

Since he didn't know either Miss Flowerdew or ghastly Gover he couldn't sensibly comment. Another silence came over them: he racked his brains for something to say. He'd never been tongue-tied with Anita before — at least, he had,

94

but that had been at the beginning, before he'd got to know her. She had certainly never been tongue-tied with him.

The silence continued. Anita smiled, rather shyly: Jamie contorted his lips. This was grotesque. He must think of something to say. He opened his mouth.

'Wha —'

'Hi, there!' said a voice. A head insinuated itself round the door: it belonged to Steven. Relief was instantaneous.

'Hi,' said Jamie.

'I trust I'm not interrupting anything? No!' Steven slid the rest of his body in the wake of his head. 'Obviously not. One on the bed, one on the floor . . . how very proper! How do you do?' He held out a hand to Anita, still kneeling on the hearth rug. 'I'm Steven Bothwell. I know who you are: you're Anita Cairncross. You'd never believe the wonderful things that I've heard about you . . .'

With the advent of Steven, conversation blossomed. It was Steven who did most of the talking, although Anita contributed her share. All Jamie did was intersperse the odd word or two. They didn't really seem to have any need of him — he wasn't at all sure that they would notice were he simply to disappear. He sat on the edge of the bed and listened to what they were saying, trying to discover for himself the art of making conversation. Anita, as always, talked about the ballet — about incidents that had happened in class, things that Miss Flowerdew had said. Steven made smart remarks and kept up his usual flow of banter. Jamie was glad to observe that Anita, although she smiled politely from time to time, was not nearly such an appreciative audience as Pauline had been. Afterwards, as he took her home, he said: 'So what did you think?'

'Of Steven? He's all right. I hear you went to a party the other night with Pauline Marshall?'

The way things got round a ballet school was nobody's business.

'It wasn't much of a do,' he said. He wondered how she'd come to hear of it. Mostly the full-time students held aloof from the part-timers, but maybe Pauline had contacts amongst them. 'I'd have asked you to come,' he said, 'except it was on Saturday and I knew you'd be going home.'

'I don't *have* to go home,' said Anita. 'I only do it because usually there isn't anything else to do.'

'Well, anyway, you didn't miss much.' He didn't really want to talk about the party, and about Pauline. 'They were all pretty ancient — two of them were Steven's girl friends.'

'He's the sort that would have two,' said Anita.

'Don't you find him amusing? Most girls seem to.'

'He's all right,' she said again.

Anita, plainly, had not been over-impressed. Steven, by contrast, the minute he arrived back at Hammersmith, greeted him with: 'That's one very superior lady you have there. I can't imagine why you waste your time chasing after all the rest of the rubbish when you could have her.'

It just went to show how little Steven knew

about anything: if he could have had Anita, he wouldn't *be* chasing after all the rest of the rubbish.

Since he couldn't have Anita he took the opportunity, next morning, of approaching number two on his list. Number two was Kate — round, bubbly Kate. Having first taken care to establish that she lived within walking distance (he wasn't running the risk of Wimbledon all over again) he magnanimously stood her a coffee in the canteen and invited her out to a meal the following Friday. She accepted with an alacrity which surprised him. (These girls really went for their food in a big way.)

'So where shall I pick you up?' he said. 'Shepherds Bush tube? About eight o'clock?'

'Super,' she said.

When he met her on Friday, she was wearing a duffle coat and jeans. She didn't look glamorous, but at least she looked approachable; that was the main thing. He took her hand as they walked back towards Hammersmith.

'Tell me,' he said, 'd'you like Chinese?'

She swung his hand.

'I like Indian.'

He hadn't asked her if she liked Indian, he'd asked her if she liked Chinese. Why did they always have to make difficulties? There was a Chinese take-away only a hundred yards down the road, near Hammersmith tube; also, he didn't happen to go a bundle on curries.

'What about Chinese?' he said.

'Chinese is all right. The only trouble is, I keep thinking of puppy dogs.'

'Puppy dogs?'

'The way they kill them and eat them.'

'Not over here,' he said. 'Not in Hammersmith.'

'How do you know?'

'Well, of course they don't!'

'But how do you *know*?'

'Well —' How *did* he know? 'Well, it'd be against the law, for a start.'

'That's no guarantee. People do things that are against the law the whole time.'

There wasn't really any arguing against that; in any case, he supposed you couldn't reasonably expect a girl to give you her all if she was worried you were making her eat puppy dogs. The least he could do was feed her a meal she felt happy with. He did rather wonder, though, why every female he encountered seemed to have some strange hang-up. First it had been naked men lying about in fields, now it was eating puppy dogs. He wondered if there were any women, anywhere, who didn't have hang-ups, or whether that was asking the impossible.

'So what sort of Indian food do you want?' he said.

She giggled.

'I only know one sort . . . that's curry.'

'So do you want chicken curry? Beef Curry? Lamb curry? Prawn curry? —'

'Not prawn curry,' said Kate.

'Egg curry? Veg. curry? Fish c —'

'Do you know,' she said, 'why it is that prawns are all pink and curled up?'

'No.' He wasn't sure that he wanted to know.

'Look, there's a tandoori place over there.'

'It's because they're thrown alive into boiling water . . . like lobsters. You mustn't ever eat them.'

'I won't; ever. I promise.' He steered her across the main road. Outside the restaurant was a sign which read FOOD TO EAT HERE OR TO TAKE AWAY. 'How about it?' he said.

Kate peered in, dubiously, through the window.

'It looks a bit grotty.'

'That's because they expect people to take stuff away,' he said. 'They don't really cater for eating on the premises. Not when it's Indian.'

She looked at him, wide-eyed.

'Why not?'

'Well, because —' He sought for a plausible reason. 'Because they don't. Not in India. I mean, you wouldn't; it'd be too hot. You'd want to go and eat on the pavement, or something. That's why they do take-aways, so you can go and eat where you want . . . if we went back to my place,' he said, 'we could listen to records.'

'Mm . . .' She pressed her nose back again against the glass. 'It certainly is very grotty in there.'

He waited for her to decide that they should go somewhere else. He ought never to have given her any choice in the matter. He should simply have marched her in and ordered two curries to take away without even consulting her. Once he'd gone and ordered the stuff she couldn't very well start making a fuss.

'All right,' she said. She peeled herself away from the glass. 'Let's take it back to your place and listen to records.'

He could hardly believe what he was hearing — she'd actually *agreed* to go *back*. It was all he could do to stop from grabbing her by the hand and rushing her off there and then. He controlled himself sufficiently to go in and order a couple of chicken curries and boiled rice, but having to wait while they were being prepared was almost unendurable. Kate kept looking round at the flock wallpaper and the pictures of the Taj Mahal and saying, 'It's not as grotty as I thought it was ... it's really quite nice, once you're inside ... I wouldn't actually have *minded* eating here. Still, I s'pose, now that we've ordered —'

'You can't chop and change,' he said. 'It gets them in a panic. And anyway, it's Friday.'

She giggled.

'What's Friday got to do with it?'

'Drunks,' said Jamie. 'All over the place. Friday night, terrible.' He snatched up the two curries and hustled her out. 'Much better at my place.'

'Is Steven going to be there?'

'No.' Had Steven been going to be there, he wouldn't have bothered asking her back. It was the very fact that Steven *wasn't* going to be there.

'I suppose,' said Kate, 'he's gone out with a girl friend?'

Jamie looked at her, suspiciously. Did he detect a wistful note?

'Actually,' he said, 'he's working late. They're doing stocktaking.'

'Oh.' She sounded surprised. 'You mean he works in a shop?'

He wondered, if he were to say 'sex shop', whether that would kill off any interest or whether it would simply serve to inflame it. He couldn't understand what it was that girls found so fascinating about Steven. It wasn't as if he were especially good-looking. He was quite reasonable-looking, but nothing out of the ordinary.

'He works in a book shop,' he said.

'Oh! A *book* shop,' said Kate.

A book shop, it seemed, was all right: a book shop was respectable. He wished now that he'd said sex shop, since that was almost certainly what it was. Kate giggled again.

'I couldn't somehow see him selling ladies' underwear!'

Little did she know. Ladies' underwear was probably the *least* of what he sold.

The room was in its usual state of chaos — mainly, it had to be said, a chaos of his own making. Steven tended to be tidy and to put things away. You could almost see a line of demarcation between his side of the room and Jamie's. Kate, fortunately, seemed not to be a girl who objected to chaos, or maybe she didn't even notice. She dropped her duffle coat on the floor, on top of a pair of tights that were waiting to be washed, helped Jamie ladle out chicken curry and rice into a couple of tin bowls, and sat down quite happily on the unmade bed to consume it.

'Want some music?' said Jamie.

The record player and the records were Steven's. Most of the records were pretty heavy stuff — electronic, and twelve tone, and all the rest. *Musique concrète*, Steven called it. It suddenly struck him:

'Concrete music . . . no wonder it's heavy.'

Kate giggled into her curry. One thing about her, she was easily amused. He sorted through the concrete music and managed to unearth a couple of pop albums. One was The Who, the other was someone called Johnny Martyr. He offered her the choice.

'The Who or Johnny Martyr . . . whoever he is.' She giggled again.

'You can't not have heard of Johnny Martyr! He's one of my favourites.'

Since he was one of her favourites, he put it on. He wasn't quite sure what he was expecting — rock, perhaps, or even punk — at any rate, something loud, with a good beat. Instead, to his disgust, he heard what sounded like a slurpy ballad drifting across the room. Really slurpy, sugary stuff, with lyrics that rhymed, like on greetings cards. He wasn't so surprised at Kate going in for syrup, but he would have thought better of Steven.

'My mum would like this,' he said.

'Would she?' said Kate; and she giggled. *Again*.

It was only after a bit that he realized why she'd giggled: on closer acquaintance, Johnny Martyr turned out to be nowhere near as innocent and slurpy as he'd seemed. He listened in growing amazement as the first number, a nauseating little ditty with the winsome title *Will you be mine?*, slowly changed from greetings card twaddle to what could only be described as soft porn. The change came about so gradually that just at first you didn't grasp what was going on.

Why spell it out? crooned Johnny Martyr.
That ain't my scene.
Give it me, baby —
You know what I mean.
I need it now,
Don't mean tomorrow —

Jamie turned wondering eyes on Kate, who giggled; *yet* again. Not that he minded her giggling quite so much now. He'd thought at first it might just be stupidity, but obviously it wasn't. Obviously, in spite of being all round and bubbly and looking so innocent, Kate knew a thing or two.

'Great, isn't it?' she said.

'Great,' said Jamie. Not exactly what you'd call *subtle* —'

Just don't withhold it from me, baby!
You know what I mean . . .

You could hardly not know what he meant; not unless you'd spent your life living in a hole in the ground.

'It gets really hairy further on,' said Kate.

Jamie lapped up his curry at a speed he normally reserved for dishes that didn't offend his palate, such as baked beans or roast beef and

Yorkshire. As a rule, with curry, he just pushed it about on his plate a bit and picked out as much of the meat as he could manage to resuscitate. Today, thanks to Johnny Martyr, he got through it without even noticing. He put his dish down on the floor.

'Want some coffee?'

Kate shook her head.

'Let's just listen to the music.'

He was quite willing. Kate lay back on the unmade bed: after a second or so, he stretched out beside her, propping himself up on one elbow. He half expected her to say 'Do you mind?' or to edge herself away, but she didn't do either; just went on lying there, eyes closed, listening to the music. Tentatively, with the hand he wasn't using for propping purposes, he stroked the side of her cheek.

'*Let's score,*' Johnny Martyr was singing, to a tune that might have come straight out of *Mary Poppins*. '*Let's you and me score, baby . . . let's score real good.*'

Jamie let his hand, as if by accident, trickle over the edge of Kate's round bubbly cheek and down the side of her neck. Under the duffle which she'd had on she was wearing a blue blouse made out of some silky material. He wondered what her reaction would be if he attempted to undo one of the buttons. When he'd tried that sort of thing with Sharon, she'd slapped his face — but then Sharon probably hadn't listened to Johnny Martyr. Knowing Sharon, she'd have pursed her lips and gone all prim at the very sound of Johnny

104

Martyr. Holding his breath, he fumbled with the top button on the blue blouse. It was rather stubborn, but it yielded at last. He waited for Kate to slap his face. Instead, she gave a little sigh and murmured: 'The side's finished.'

Sod the side. Sides were always finishing at the most inconvenient of moments.

'Aren't you going to turn it over?'

He supposed he would have to. She'd only lie there nagging about it if he didn't. Just so long as she didn't get *up*.

She didn't get up. When he climbed back on to the bed she was not only still lying there, but had actually left the button undone. He couldn't believe his luck: she was practically *asking* him for it.

Under the blue blouse she was wearing a blue bra with little blue forget-me-nots embroidered all over it. He wondered if she'd put it on specially. It didn't look like the sort of garment she'd wear every day — at least, he wouldn't have thought that it did, but then he wasn't exactly an expert. He didn't know all that much about girls' undergarments. Kim hadn't yet reached the stage of wearing bras, and his mother's, when he'd seen them on the line, had been all white and flapping.

He slid down again, by Kate's side. This time, he didn't prop himself up on one elbow but lay down properly. Kate, obligingly, wriggled closer. A strong aroma of scent assailed his nostrils; roses, or lilies of the valley, or some such thing. In spite of the duffle and the jeans, she'd obviously gone to no small amount of trouble. He wished now that he'd had the forethought to help himself to some of Steven's perfumed deodorant. He didn't *think* that he smelt — he'd had a good wash before going to meet her — but he would have liked to be certain.

He obviously didn't; or if he did, she hadn't noticed it. Or didn't care. Whichever, she made no objection to his kissing her. Not only made no objection but actively participated, which was a change from some girls. Some girls just pouted their lips and seemed to think that was all that was required. It wasn't any fun kissing a girl who did that.

He slid an experimental hand inside the neck of Kate's blouse. (Johnny Martyr was now singing of things unmentionable.) Kate let it remain there. She ran her fingers through his hair and a pleasurable prickling went shooting all the way down his spine.

. . . till I scream, crooned Johnny Martyr.

Kate gave a little shiver. She took his hand and firmly guided it inside her blue bra with the embroidered forget-me-nots. Jamie swallowed. This was the furthest he'd ever got with any girl.

It seemed it was the furthest he was destined to get (for this evening, at any rate). As the second side of Johnny Martyr drooled to its end, Kate suddenly sprang up on the bed.

'I think I ought to go now,' she said.

'Go?' He was flabbergasted. What did she mean, go? Go where? His immediate thought was that she must mean, go to the bathroom. It took a

106

second or so for the truth to sink in.

'Go home.' Feverishly, she was re-arranging her bra, doing up the buttons of her blouse. He watched her, still flabbergasted.

'What d'you want to go home for? It's only —' he took a quick look at his watch — 'only quarter to ten. You don't want to go home at quarter to ten.'

He put his arms about her, trying to coax her back. For a moment he thought she was going to yield, but then, determinedly, she broke away.

'No, I must,' she said. 'Really. Before we go too far.'

That flabbergasted him even more. She lay there, letting him undo her blouse, putting his hand on her breast, listening to some slob of a pop star singing pornographic songs, and then she dared to talk about *going too far*? He pushed his hair out of his eyes. This was unbelievable.

'I'm sorry,' said Kate. She looked at him, earnestly, all giggles gone. 'Really I am. It's not that I wouldn't *like* to. It's just that I never *have* —'

That made two of them, he thought.

'There's always a first time,' he said.

'Oh, yes; I *know*. And I keep thinking about it — I keep *meaning* to. But then, when it comes to it —'

Then when it came to it, she went and got cold feet. Or cold something else.

'I wouldn't let anything happen to you,' he said. 'I mean . . . we'd take precautions.'

'Yes, I *know*.'

'You'd be quite safe.'

107

'Yes, I *know*.'

'Then why —'

Kate thrust her fingers into her hair and tugged, in a kind of apologetic frenzy.

'I don't *know*. It's just that when it *comes* to it —'

She'd said that already.

'— I'm not really, absolutely, one hundred per cent certain that I actually *want* to. I mean, I *do* want to — but then again I *don't*. And I don't think that until one *does* — I mean, a hundred per cent absolutely *certainly* — well, I don't think that one *ought*. Do you?' She looked at him, pleading. 'I mean, I know there *are* girls — I mean, Natalie.' Big blonde Natalie. 'Natalie does it all the time, practically with anyone. Well, not exactly *any*one. But anyone she fancies. I mean, she doesn't have to be in *love* with them, or anything . . .' Her voice trailed off. 'Oh, Jamie, I *am* sorry,' she said. '*Really* I am. I do hope it hasn't upset you, or anything.'

Upset him? Oh, no. He *liked* people leading him on. He *enjoyed* that kind of thing. A little bit of frustration was good for you every now and again.

'I do feel awful,' said Kate. (*She* felt awful?) 'I feel I'm taking advantage of you — being so nice-natured, and everything. If you weren't so nice-natured, I wouldn't dare.'

She'd better be warned: he didn't feel so nice-natured. Not just at this moment.

'I mean,' she said. She looked round, big-eyed, at the room. 'You could cut my throat or stick a poker up me or almost *anything*.'

Fat lot of satisfaction that would give him.

'It must be your lucky day,' he said. 'I haven't got a poker.'

Kate giggled, though a trifle nervously. He knew she wasn't nervous of him turning physical — what with him being so nice-natured, and all — but nervous, nonetheless, in case he was mad at her. He wondered whether he was. He thought about it for a bit, and decided that on the whole it wasn't worth the effort. There really didn't seem much point. He could yell at her and call her by a few names, but where was that going to get him? She was all done up, now, and ready to go home. Yelling at her wasn't likely to make her change her mind.

'I'd better take the record off,' he said.

He bet Johnny Martyr didn't have this trouble with women. He glared resentfully at the photograph on the sleeve. Great grinning buffoon. Some ponce *he* looked, with all his rings and baubles.

'I'll make some coffee,' he said.

He only did it to keep up the image of his nice nature. Kate kept saying, 'Oh, Jamie, I am sorry, *honestly*,' but he didn't want to hear it any more. He wasn't sulking, or being mad at her, or anything like that, it was just that the moment had passed: he wasn't interested. He'd been interested five minutes ago, and no doubt he'd be interested again the minute she'd gone; but right now, as at this particular moment in time, he couldn't be bothered. If it hadn't been for demonstrating the niceness of his nature, he'd just as soon have taken her back home straight away.

At quarter past ten, as they were leaving, Steven arrived back.

'Hallo, 'allo, 'allo!' he said. 'And what have we here? Fair Kathleen, an' I am not mistaken — had yourselves a good time?'

'Smashing,' said Jamie. 'We played your Johnny Martyr.'

Steven laughed.

'That fat queen!'

Downstairs, in the street, Kate said in worried tones: 'You don't think it's true, do you?'

'Don't think what's true?'

'What Steven said . . . about Johnny Martyr being a queen.'

''Course it is,' said Jamie. 'You can tell, just by looking at him. Spot it a mile off.'

He dropped her off in Shepherds Bush (Victorian: end of terrace: smart side of street. Shutters at the windows, shrubs in pots) and because of his nice nature forced himself to wait while she searched through all her pockets for her front door key.

'Thank you ever so much for the meal,' she said. 'It was really nice. And I am sorry about — you know.'

' 'Sall right,' said Jamie.

'No, but I am,' said Kate. 'Really.' She found her key at last and inserted it in the lock. 'See you in class tomorrow?'

'Yeah,' he said. 'See ya.'

On the way back to Hammersmith he was approached by a lady in a fur coat and high heels. He thought she was going to ask him the time, or how to get somewhere. Instead, as she drew level with him, she winked and said, 'Hallo, darling . . . want to learn a thing or two?' Politely he said that he didn't; not just at this moment, thank you. The lady shrugged.

'Oh, well, suit yourself,' she said.

And why shouldn't he? It was what everybody else seemed to do. From now on, he intended to be *ruthless*.

6

In March, the auditions were held for the forth-
coming September. They were held on a Friday
morning, which meant Jamie had to take time off
from Plumber's to attend. For the whole of the
past week he'd been having his leg pulled by
Charlie and Big Mac, to the accompaniment of
sundry disgruntled remarks from Dennis on the
subject of people that got given grants to ponce
around dancing while the rest of them had to put
their shoulders to the wheel and earn a living.
(Dennis had recently applied for the post of head
basement man in Oxford Street and been turned
down on grounds of lack of experience, as a result
of which he was feeling a trifle jaundiced with
life.) Jamie was surprised, therefore, on Thursday evening, to be solemnly presented with a
card bearing the picture of a black cat with a
horseshoe round its neck and the message, in
Charlie's hand-writing: 'All the best with the
ordition'. It had been signed not only by Charlie
and Big Mac but by Dennis, as well. Jamie
stammered his thanks, embarrassed in the face of
such unexpected goodwill.

'Don't mention it,' said Charlie. 'Least we could do.'

'But you just remember,' said Dennis. 'You just remember, when you're up there with all the nobs, gettin' your picture in the papers and appearing on the telly, you just remember it was us down 'ere as started you off.'

That was too much. He felt moved to make a protest:

'I haven't even passed the audition yet!'

'You'd better,' said Charlie. 'We're counting on it . . .'

The audition, basically, was just an ordinary class, except that they were joined by six boys from other schools and were watched from the far end of the room by Miss Gover (ghastly Gover), Miss Flowerdew and the Hun, who sat solemnly at a table making notes. The class was taken by a foreign man with a name that sounded like someone sneezing. ('Alex Kaszubowsky,' said Anita. 'He's super!')

Afterwards, they were called in one at a time to be interviewed by the panel of adjudicators, now reinforced by the sneezing man, who had also taken his seat at the table. Since they were called in alphabetical order, Jamie was second to go in, after Steven.

'What's it like?' he said.

Steven shrugged.

'All right . . . if you don't mind being put through the third degree.'

It wasn't quite as bad as all that, but he began

to see what Anita had meant about Miss Gover. She was elderly and tight-lipped, and wore gold-rimmed spectacles attached to a chain. Her expression was supercilious: even just saying his name she managed to inject a note of scorn.

'James Carr,' she said; and he almost expected to see four pairs of lips curl up in derision. 'Seventeen years and one month . . . studied with Thea Tucker . . . now taking evening classes here at Kendra Hall.'

Miss Gover seemed to be the one who was in charge, because it was she who did most of the talking and asked most of the questions, like what had made him take up ballet in the first place, and why he hadn't started till he was sixteen, and what made him think he wanted to be a dancer. He'd known they were probably going to ask him that, and he still hadn't come up with any satisfactory reply. He couldn't very well say it was because he was unable to think of anything else.

'I expect partly it's because you enjoy dancing,' suggested Miss Flowerdew, trying to be helpful. Miss Flowerdew was younger than Miss Gover, and far less forbidding. She had wavy brown hair and an encouraging smile.

'Well?' said Miss Gover. '*Do* you enjoy dancing?'

'He does,' said the Hun. 'I can vouch for that.'

Jamie nearly fell off his seat in amazement. The *Hun*? Putting in a good word for someone?

'Why do you enjoy it?' said Miss Gover.

'Well —' He scraped his throat. 'I guess because it's the thing I do best.'

Coldly, Miss Gover regarded him.

'Really?' she said.

'Yeah, really,' said Jamie. It was one point he was very certain of.

'And simply because it's the thing you do best —' her voice was definitely sneering — 'you think that makes you good enough to be a professional?'

'I dunno about that,' he said. 'But I wouldn't mind giving it a go.'

Miss Gover's eyebrows disappeared one after another into her hairline. Miss Flowerdew smiled, and the sneezing man twitched slightly. The Hun leaned forward across the table.

'Tell me,' he said. 'Dancing's the thing you're best at, but what other things do you do? What else are you good at?'

'Cricket,' said Jamie. 'Football. Swimming —'

'Academically,' said Miss Gover. She bent her head and looked down, through her gold-rimmed spectacles, at the sheet of paper she had before her. He remembered Old Joe, in his study at school. 'Only three CSEs, I see — and you haven't studied music at all?'

He could have told her about the band at infant school, when he'd played the triangle and Doug had bashed the drum (just for a couple of weeks, until they'd discovered their mistake and taken him off it) but somehow he didn't think she'd be too impressed.

'I've got a trumpet,' he said. Chinese, with a defective valve. 'I can play that.'

'Indeed?' said Miss Gover.

'I believe trumpets are quite difficult?' That was Miss Flowerdew again. 'I believe they take quite a lof of playing?'

Especially when they had defective valves. He'd never really learnt to do more than make noises.

'Suppose you don't dance,' said the sneezing man. 'What do you do instead?'

That was a lousy question. Work in the basement at Plumber's?

'I had thought of playing cricket,' he said, 'but then I went and got chucked off the team for not attending practice. The reason I wasn't attending practice —' he looked Miss Gover straight in the eye as he said it — 'was because I was going to these rehearsals for Miss Tucker. They said I had to choose; either cricket or ballet.'

'So you chose ballet?' said the Hun. He grinned. 'That must have made you popular!'

Strange how the most inhuman of people suddenly turned out to be human after all. The Hubbard, the Hun — he didn't know about Miss Gover. He had his doubts about her.

'Well,' she was saying, briskly putting his papers away in a folder, 'I think that will be all for the moment. Unless anyone else has any questions they'd like to ask —?' It appeared that no one had. 'In that case,' said Miss Gover, 'it only remains to say thank you for coming along, and we shall, of course, let you know.'

Miss Flowerdew came to the door to see him off.

'It'll take about four weeks,' she whispered.

116

'But don't worry . . . we'll be in touch as soon as possible.'

He had lunch in the canteen with Anita and Miss Tucker, who had brought along two of her younger pupils to audition for the junior school.

'They're in there now,' she said. 'Nervous as kittens. One will get in; I don't hold out much hope for the other. Of course —' she gave Jamie one of her penetrating looks — 'you'll have had no difficulty.'

He wished everyone wouldn't keep taking it for granted. It was going to make it all the harder if he failed.

'Nonsense!' said Miss Tucker. 'I have received excellent reports of you.'

'But that Miss Gover,' he said. 'I don't reckon she went for me.'

'Do not presume to judge.' Miss Tucker raised her glass of water to her lips. 'There is a child over there,' she said, 'who appears to be trying to attract your attention.'

Jamie looked; so did Anita. The child was Pauline. She beamed, and waved at him across the canteen. Jamie waved back.

'Girl in my class,' he said.

As he was finishing his first course (jacket potato and cauliflower cheese) Kate came by the table. She stopped, and dimpled.

'Hallo, Jamie . . . how was the audition?'

'Not bad,' he said. 'How about you?'

She rolled her eyes.

'*Fear*some . . . if I get in, I'll stand you that Chinese meal we never had.'

117

'I'll hold you to it.'

Anita waited till Kate was out of earshot.

'Another girl in your class?' she said.

With the auditions over, and a fortnight's break in classes almost upon them, he was able to turn his attention back to that other little matter of importance in his life: namely, his list. There were only two names left on it by now, sexy Natalie and foxy Doreen. He couldn't make up his mind which one to go for. In theory, it should have been Natalie, since Doreen was only down as reserve, but he kept thinking about what Kate had said: *Natalie does it all the time. Practically with anyone* ... Did he really want to do it with someone who did it all the time? Practically with anyone? He wasn't sure that he did. He was growing pretty desperate, but not as desperate as all that, and in any case, just recently he had noticed that Doreen was showing distinct signs of a thaw towards him. She didn't snap as much as she used to, and she hadn't said 'Do you mind?' for ages. In the event the matter was decided for him by Natalie suddenly announcing, as they limbered up before classes next day, that she was going away for Easter.

'One of the girls in my flat knows this super guy who has a cottage in Norfolk ... we're all going down there in his car for a fortnight.'

That settled it: he couldn't afford to sit around doing nothing for a whole fortnight. Time was precious. He was about to ask Doreen if she was doing anything during the break, when she pre-empted him.

'Ask me where I'm going for Easter . . . go on! Ask me!'

His heart sank. It looked as though he were going to have to sit around doing nothing whether he liked it or not.

'Where are you going for Easter?'

Doreen gave a little snort of laughter.

'Acton-on-Sea!'

He thought at first that she meant Clacton; and then he got it.

'Acton?' Acton was almost as close as Shepherds Bush . . . 'That where you live?'

'Well, I wouldn't go there for a holiday, would I?' said Doreen. 'Nobody would go to Acton for a *holiday.*'

He played it very cool with Doreen. He quickly discovered that her favourite pastime was walking round the shops. She preferred it if they were open and she could go and walk round inside, but even if they were closed she still got a buzz out of it. What she liked was to choose outfits for herself. She chose outfits for every conceivable occasion (plus some which if you asked him were pretty *in*conceivable). She chose them for when she got married to some famous personage, such as John McEnroe or a member of the Royal Family; she chose them for when she went to first-night parties, given in her honour; for when she flew to Hollywood to play Anna Pavlova; for when she appeared on television chat shows; even, for goodness' sake, for when she went to Buckingham Palace to get her OBE. You had to be prepared, she explained, for every eventuality. What amazed him was that she seemed to remember every single garment she'd ever clapped eyes on. She had a mind like a filing cabinet.

'If I put that dress with that coat we saw in Peter Jones . . . if I wore those shoes with that hat they had in Selfridge's . . .'

As a reward for tramping the streets — Oxford Street, Bond Street, Regent Street, Knightsbridge — she let him kiss her on the doorstep when he delivered her back home (sixth floor flat, high rise council block). He couldn't take her back to Hammersmith, because Steven was there. As far as he could make out, Steven was always going to be there. He'd obviously stopped fancying either Sue or Emilia and hadn't yet found himself anyone else — didn't seem to be trying very hard, either. It was really rather a nuisance. It cramped his style, having Steven always about. He wondered, if he were to put it to her nicely, whether Doreen would come away with him to a hotel. He'd never been to a hotel before, but as he'd said to Kate, there was always a first time.

Surreptitiously, down in the basement, he sounded out Charlie.

'I know a hotel,' said Charlie. 'Dirt cheap, no questions asked. Five minutes from King's Cross.'

'I don't think she'd go for King's Cross,' said Jamie. It was hardly the sort of area that would appeal to a girl who had visions of marrying into royalty and getting the OBE. 'I'd thought of somewhere more like . . . well . . . Richmond, or somewhere.'

'I dunno about Richmond,' said Charlie. 'That's outside my manor, that is.'

In the end, he bought a local paper and discovered a hotel called The Pack Horse which advertised itself as being 'down by the river'. She'd like it down by the river; she could go and choose a river outfit for herself. Greatly daring, from a pay telephone in Plumber's, he rang The Pack Horse and inquired the price of a double room for one night. He felt like something out of a blue movie. It was one thing taking a girl back home to listen to records; quite another booking a room in a hotel. Somehow, it felt incredibly pornographic. The sort of thing he definitely wouldn't want his mother to know about.

The price of the room staggered him. He could have lived for a week on just the price of that one room. Still, he reckoned at that sort of money it would have to be good, which was just as well because old foxy Doreen was really quite fastidious. He'd discovered that over these last few days of tramping around. She wouldn't drink from a cracked cup or eat off a dirty plate or anything like that. The least little speck and back it would go, it didn't matter where she was, a coffee bar in Hammersmith or some posh place in the West End. She had standards, did Doreen, and he couldn't see her lowering them just for him, even though she did let him kiss her good night. Once when the lift had been empty on its way up to the sixth floor, she had even let him do a bit more than just kiss, which had encouraged him to hope, though after Kate he didn't place too much dependence on girls necessarily meaning what you thought they meant.

On the Saturday evening before classes were due to start again, they tramped down Knightsbridge in search of something to go with something she'd seen on Thursday, when they'd tramped the length of Oxford Street amongst the late-night shoppers. He was sick to death of tramping streets.

'You know over Easter you just stayed at Acton-on-Sea?' he said.

'Yes,' said Doreen. 'What d'you think about that little black jacket? That might go with it.'

'Yeah,' he said. 'Smashing. I was wondering if you'd like to come away somewhere for the night.'

'It might make me look too old,' said Doreen. 'That's the only trouble. It's very difficult to tell, when you can't try things on.'

'I thought maybe next Saturday, after class.'

'What? Go away?' She turned at last from the shop window to look at him. 'You and me?'

'I thought it would be fun. Make up for Easter.'

'But where would we go?'

'There's this hotel I've found,' said Jamie. 'Down by the river. Near Richmond. Dead classy.'

Doreen considered him a while.

'You mean —' he'd noticed before, she was a girl who liked to get things straight — 'you mean, sleep in the same bedroom?'

122

'Well — yes.' That *was* what he meant; definitely.

Doreen considered him a bit more.

'Are we going to be married?' she said.

He recoiled at that. Who'd said anything about marriage? Then he twigged: people who went away together to hotels always signed the register as Mr and Mrs. It had been very naïve of him not to have thought of that for himself.

'I s'pose we'll have to,' he said.

'Jamie!' Doreen flung both arms round him. 'Now I can go and choose an *engagement* outfit!'

He was a bit nervous about that: so long as it was only one of her imaginary ones . . .

'We'll have to get a ring,' she said. She sounded really happy about it. 'I'll get the wedding ring, you get the engagement ring.'

'What do we want an engagement ring for?'

'Because you can't have one without the other, stupid! It would look ridiculous.'

'Oh. Would it?'

'Of course it would! Don't you know anything?'

Not about engagement rings, he didn't.

'What sort of thing have I got to get, then?'

'Oh, anything'll do for now — so long as it looks like a proper engagement ring. But you don't have to spend a fortune. Not if you can't afford it. We can always get something better later on.'

He wondered what she meant by later on. If they went away a second time, he supposed.

Doreen tucked her arm through his.

'Isn't it fun? It's the sort of thing they do stories on . . . *Partners in Ballet — Partners in Real Life* . . . it's really romantic.' She sighed, contentedly, and snuggled closer. 'I always thought you were romantic. Right from the very beginning.'

He didn't know what to say to that. He couldn't very well say he'd thought she was romantic right from the very beginning. After all, he'd only put her down as reserve. If one of Natalie's flatmates hadn't known someone with a cottage in Norfolk, it might have been Natalie coming with him to The Pack Horse.

On Monday evening after class he experienced a rather embarrassing moment. Doreen had hung around waiting for him (the girls finished half an hour earlier than the boys: they usually clustered in a gaggle in a nearby coffee bar) and in front of the Hun and all the rest of them threw her arms about him and pressed a fond peck on his cheek. Were he in the habit of blushing, he would have blushed. Fortunately he wasn't, but still he could have done without quite such a public display. He disentangled himself, to the predictable accompaniment of jeers and catcalls. Doreen didn't seem to mind them — she even seemed quite pleased.

'Have you got it?' she whispered.

'Got what?'

'*You know* . . . the *ring*.'

'Oh.' The ring; it had completely slipped his memory. 'No, not yet. I'll get it on Friday.'

'Not till then?'

'Well, we're not going —' he lowered his

voice — 'we're not going away till Saturday.'

'You'd better get it,' said Doreen. 'I'm not coming without.'

'I'll get it.'

'A real engagement ring . . . I don't mind if it's not expensive, but it's got to be *real*.'

'Yeah, OK.' He wasn't quite sure what constituted a 'real' engagement ring, but presumably Woolworth's would sell them. It was only for one night, after all: he could hardly afford to *keep* taking her away, he was going to be living on chipolatas again as it was. He had never realized the pursuit of experience would come so dear.

'My mother says,' said Doreen, 'that you'd better come round on Friday night and have a meal with us.'

She issued it not so much as an invitation as an order. He wondered why Doreen's mother, all of a sudden, should feel the need to meet him.

'Well, it's obvious, isn't it?' said Doreen. 'In the circumstances.'

He looked at her, askance.

'You haven't gone and told her?'

'Of course I've told her! She's my mother, isn't she?'

'Yeah, but —'

Words failed him. He tried to imagine telling *his* mother he was taking a girl away to a hotel for a night. All hell would be let loose. 'You mean she doesn't mind?'

'She'd rather we waited,' said Doreen. 'She thinks we're a bit young. On the other hand, *she* was only eighteen, so she can't really say very much.'

'She told you that?' he said. 'She *told* you she was only eighteen?'

'Well, I knew anyway,' said Doreen. 'It's hardly any secret.'

Bloody hell!

'She said as far as she's concerned, if we've really made up our minds then we'd better go ahead — but obviously she wants to meet you. That's only natural.'

It didn't seem natural to him. It would have seemed more natural to him if the old girl had turned up at Kendra Hall with a rolling pin, threatening to beat the living daylights out of him. He reckoned that's what Mr Carr would do if Kim ever came home and said some yob was taking her off for the night. Maybe it was something to do with the fact that Doreen hadn't any father. (He'd run away when she was ten, she said, with a girl from the United Dairies where he worked.) Maybe not having any man in the house, Mrs Willis had forgotten what they were like. Maybe she thought he was just taking her daughter away, out of the kindness of his heart, to give her a day's break from Acton. Immoral Purposes probably hadn't even crossed her mind.

'Come round at seven,' said Doreen. 'And *don't forget to bring the ring.*'

'No,' he said. He was still feeling a bit bemused. 'OK.'

During the course of the week it came to his notice that neither Kate nor Pauline was smiling at him any more. He bumped into them in the corridor one evening, as they were coming out of the girls' changing room together, and they just sniffed, in unison, and walked straight past without so much as a word. He discovered why later on in the evening when Steven winked at him and said: 'So we've gone and got ourselves engaged, have we?'

Was the woman *mad*? Next thing he knew, she'd be announcing it in the papers.

'It was what you might call expedient,' he said.

'Well, I gathered that,' said Steven. 'You might be green, but you're not stupid.'

'Thanks very much,' said Jamie.

Friday lunchtime he went into Woolworth's and bought a ring for eighty pence. It wasn't much of a ring, but it fitted his little finger when he tried it on (Doreen had said that was how he was to test it for size) and it glittered quite nicely when it caught the light. From a distance no one would know that it wasn't real diamonds.

He wore his collar and tie for meeting Doreen's mother. In his experience, mothers liked collars and ties; it seemed to give them a sense of security. People who wore collars and ties were respectable: people who wore sweat shirts and jeans were into sex and drugs and all the other things they didn't approve of.

Duly at seven o'clock he presented himself at the front door of the Willis's flat. In his hand he was clutching a bunch of flowers he'd picked from the back garden in Hammersmith. He didn't know what they were — weeds, in all probability; they were a bit mangy — but it was the thought that counted. That was what Mrs Carr was always saying: 'It's not the money, it's the thought that counts.'

Doreen opened the door to him. The first thing she said was: 'Have you got it?'

'Yeah —'

He held out his hand for her to see. In her eagerness, she almost yanked his little finger off.

'Has he got it?'

Mrs Willis had appeared, at the far end of the narrow hallway. She looked disconcertingly like an older version of Doreen: she had the same wispy red hair and slightly foxy expression.

'Well?' she said. Her voice was thin, and rather on the sharp side. 'Where is it?'

'Here.' Doreen stretched out her hand, proudly displaying the Woolworth's ring. Mrs Willis peered at it.

'Tinfoil,' she said.

'Doesn't matter.' Doreen turned her hand, trying to catch the light. 'We can always get another later on.'

'Just so long as you do,' said Mrs Willis. She nodded towards Jamie, still standing at the front door. 'So you're the young man, are you? I'm Doreen's mother. You'd better come in where I can take a look at you.'

They sat down in the tiny kitchen to a meal of fish and chips and tinned peaches and custard. It wasn't the sort of meal you got at Anita's, but at least he knew what to do with it. The few times he'd eaten at Anita's he'd lived in fear of tackling the wrong bit of food at the wrong time, or the right bit of food the wrong way. (Like artichokes. He defied anyone who'd never had an artichoke to know what to do with them. *He* hadn't known you had to pull them to pieces and suck.)

'And where did you go to school?' said Mrs Willis. She'd already asked him what his father did, and what sort of place they lived in, and whether he had any brothers or sisters. He supposed she was just interested rather than nosy, but the way she shot the questions at him, one after another, pop-pop-pop, as if they were on a check list, definitely gave him the feeling that he was being grilled. Still, he supposed she had to make certain. She wouldn't want her daughter to go away with just anyone. (It still amazed him that she was willing to let her go away at all.)

'Jamie,' said Doreen. 'My mother asked you a question.'

'Sorry!' He snapped to attention. 'I've forgotten what it was.'

'Where you went to school,' said Doreen.

'Oh, yes.' He wondered whether he could get away with saying Eton or Harrow. Probably not. He racked his brain, trying to remember where it was that Steven had gone. Something House — Something Park — Something —

'*Well?*'

They were waiting; watching him as they did so.

'Er — Tenterden Road Comprehensive,' he said.

'That's all right, then.' Mrs Willis held out a

hand for his empty plate. 'It doesn't do to have too great a disparity. These things always stand more chance if people come from similar sorts of backgrounds. Leastways, that's the way I see it.' She took away the custard dish and replaced it with a packet of After Eight. 'I'll make some coffee. I like it with hot milk, and so does Doreen. You'll have to start getting used to all her little habits from now on, you know.'

She said this humorously — at least, he thought she did. He laughed, not quite certain.

'Oh, yes,' said Mrs Willis. 'It's not all a bed of roses, I can tell you. You'll find she's got some funny little ways.'

'Mum! For heaven's sake!' Doreen pulled a face at Jamie across the table. 'Don't start on that . . . Jamie doesn't want to be put off before we've even done it.'

She was actually talking out loud about *doing* it — in front of her own mother. He couldn't believe it; this was extraordinary. He didn't know people had mothers that were that liberated.

'Well, I don't know,' said Mrs Willis. She clattered a milk bottle out of the refrigerator. 'It's all a bit sudden, if you ask me. You've hardly known each other five minutes.'

'*Mum*,' said Doreen. She said it warningly. 'You *promised*.'

'I know I did. It's just that seeing him —' She turned, and looked at Jamie. 'You're such children.'

'Old enough,' said Doreen. 'Look at you.'

'I was eighteen — and your father was twenty-one.' She jerked the milk bottle in Jamie's direction. 'He hasn't even started shaving.'

'*Mum!*' shrieked Doreen.

'Oh, very well!' Mrs Willis snatched up a saucepan from the draining board and began slopping milk into it. 'I've had my say. You know what my feelings are.'

She set the saucepan on the gas and put the remains of the milk back in the refrigerator. When she turned round again she had a look of tight-lipped resignation on her face.

'All I can say is, don't come running to me when things go wrong . . . I had to learn the hard way: you'll have to do the same. What do *your* parents have to say?'

'My parents?' He was taken off balance. 'Well, I — I haven't actually mentioned it to them.'

'Then I suggest, young man, that you do! And with all speed! You can't go ahead with a thing like this without consulting your parents. Suppose they don't happen to like the idea? Or hadn't that occurred to you?'

'Er — well —' He floundered.

Mrs Willis reached into a cupboard for the instant coffee.

'When exactly,' she said, 'were you planning it for?'

The question was addressed specifically to Jamie. He cast an anguished eye in Doreen's direction. (He thought she was supposed to have *told* her?)

'I said,' said Doreen. 'We haven't yet fixed any definite date.'

What?

'Well, if you ask me,' said Mrs Willis, 'the longer it's left the better. In my opinion, twenty-five is about the right age.'

Twenty-*five*? Was she *crazy*?

He got out as fast as he could, at half past nine.

'Thanks for the meal,' he said. 'It was terrific.'

'We've never stinted on food,' said Mrs Willis. 'Heaven only knows how you're going to manage on a grant.'

The remark puzzled him. It was nice of her to worry about how he was going to manage, but he couldn't for the life of him think why she should. He hadn't exactly got the impression she'd gone overboard about him.

She came to the door to see him off.

'Just don't be in too much of a hurry,' she said. 'That's my advice.'

Doreen, fondly, said that she would see him down in the lift so that he could see her back up again.

'It's usually empty at this time of night.'

It was empty, but he was feeling too confused to take advantage of it. He clanged the gate shut behind them.

'I thought you told me,' he said, 'that you'd told her?'

'What are you talking about?' said Doreen. 'I did tell her. You heard her, carrying on.'

'Yeah, but she was carrying on about waiting till we're twenty-five.'

'Oh, well! That's just her.'

'But she didn't seem to *know*.'

'Know what, for goodness' sake?' Doreen looked at him, rather irritably. 'What are you talking about?'

'About tomorrow!'

'I didn't tell her *that*. What d'you think, I'm daft or something? I told her I'm going to stay with a girl friend. She'd do her nut if she thought I was going away with you.'

The lift stopped at the third floor and a couple of girls got in. Doreen stood twisting her hand to and fro, trying to flash her eighty pence ring: Jamie stood watching her, trying to work things out. Something very odd was going on here. He couldn't understand it. (He wasn't too sure that he wanted to understand it.)

They reached the ground floor and the two girls got out. He was almost tempted to follow them, but already Doreen had slammed the door shut and pressed the button for the fifteenth floor.

'Might as well go all the way.' She giggled. 'Here . . . that was a joke!'

'Yeah; I got it.'

'I bought the wedding ring,' said Doreen. 'It's real silver — cost me £8.50. I used my savings.'

The sweat broke out all over him.

'I bet this didn't cost £8.50.' She stretched out her left hand, fingers splayed. 'It looks really cheap . . . we'll have to get another one some time.'

'What —' He cleared his throat. 'What do we want another one for?'

'Well, you don't think I'm going to wear *this* for the rest of my life?'

'It's only for one night,' he said. 'You can chuck it after that.'

There was a long silence. Doreen's lips had suddenly gone all pinched and thin.

'What exactly do you mean?' she said. 'It's only for one night?'

'Well, what I mean ... it's very expensive going to hotels.'

'So what?' said Doreen, coldly.

'Well, like I said . . . it's very expensive.'

'I heard you the first time! I don't see what that's got to do with me having a proper engagement ring.'

'People only have proper engagement rings,' he said, desperately, 'when they're properly engaged. After all, it's only the one night, isn't it?'

'Is it?' said Doreen.

'That's what we agreed on — it's what I booked for. It's what I *said*.'

'You said,' said Doreen, 'that we were going to be married.'

'Yeah, well . . . just for the occasion.'

'Are you mad?' said Doreen. Now her voice had gone all pinched and thin, like her lips. 'Do you really imagine that I would come away with you to a *hotel* and sleep in the same *bed*room in the same *bed* unless we were going to be *married*? *Properly*? What do you think? I'm a *whore*, or something? Is that why you bought me a cheap ring? Because you think that's all I'm *worth*?'

This was like a nightmare. He couldn't understand how it had happened.

134

'I think there's been a bit of a misunderstanding,' he said.

'I should think there has been a bit of a misunderstanding! *You're* the one that's done all the misunderstanding. You're just like all the rest of them . . . only after one thing! I thought you were different — I thought you were *decent*. Well, you're not, you're horrible!'

'No, I'm not,' he said. He refused to be called horrible just because there'd been a misunderstanding.

'Yes, you are!' said Doreen. 'You're *horrible*. Telling everyone you're going to marry me then suddenly backing out at the last minute.'

'I'm not backing out at the last minute!'

'*Oh*?' said Doreen. '*Aren't* you?'

'No! I never said —'

'You said we were going to be married! You either meant it or you didn't.'

'I did mean it — but just for the night! Just the one night.'

'People do not get married,' said Doreen, witheringly, 'just for the one night. They get married in sickness or in health till death them do part.'

'Unless they get divorced,' he said.

'You can't get divorced,' screamed Doreen, 'if you've never been married! You can take back your rotten lousy ring —' she tore it off her finger and hurled it down at his feet — 'it's cheap and it's nasty and I wouldn't be seen *dead* in it!' The lift came to a halt at the fifteenth floor. 'And you can get out *here*,' said Doreen, 'and *walk*.'

In a daze, he got out. Doreen's voice came

screeching after him: 'If I wanted, I could have you up for breach of *promise*.'

The lift door clanged shut; the lift disappeared. Abandoned on the fifteenth floor, Jamie shook his head: he *still* didn't understand how it had happened.

7

The following week, Doreen went round telling everyone who would listen that she'd been jilted. Jamie only knew about it because Steven told him, Steven being always bang up to date with the latest gossip. None of the girls made any mention of it, though he'd noticed that Kate and Pauline were smiling at him again. Now he knew the reason why. They'd been mad at him for being (as they thought) engaged: they were happy with him now that he no longer was. Nobody, curiously enough, seemed to hold it against him. He would have thought that girls being girls they would all have ganged up and ostracized him, but in fact Doreen was the only one who practised ostracism. When she saw him in the corridor she walked straight past as if he were invisible: when he tried talking to her in the canteen, in a bid to re-establish normal relations, she simply went deaf and refused to acknowledge that he had spoken. Or, indeed, that he was even *there*.

He hadn't realized at first that she was doing it, because Saturday morning, when they should have had the Hun for pas de deux, Alex Kaszu-bowsky turned up instead and for some reason best known to himself decided to have a grand re-shuffling of partners. Since there were more girls than boys in the class, some of the boys — not Percy, because he was a midget, and not Graham, because he still had a tendency to flow about (not to mention a tendency to drop people) — were allotted two females each. Jamie now found himself with Pauline, which was when he first noticed that she was smiling at him again, and Natalie. Doreen was shunted off on to Graham, which served her right. Not that he knew, at that stage, that she was running about telling people that he'd jilted her, but it was enough that he'd had to forfeit the deposit on the hotel room. They'd insisted on a deposit. He hadn't known whether it was standard practice, or whether it was because they'd suspected from his telephone voice that he was still green as grass, but in any case he'd been too anxious, at the time, to query it. He'd meekly sent off the money, and now, thanks to Ms Willis, had had to forfeit it. He didn't mind shelling out when you got something in return, but he did object to wastage.

Pauline, quite definitely, was feeling happy with him again.

'Been to any good parties lately?' she said, at the end of class.

He grunted.

'Gone off parties.'

'That's a pity. I know someone who's giving

one. This Friday . . . Collier's Wood.'

She looked at him, enticingly. She still had this little cheeky elfin face. He forced himself to remember that she also had hang-ups about naked men lying around in fields — and where for crying out loud was Collier's Wood? He couldn't keep forking out on tube fares here there and everywhere, right to the furthest flung edges of the underground system.

'It's not far,' said Pauline, encouragingly. 'Catch the train from South Wimbledon, it's only one stop up.'

South Wimbledon; that did it. He wasn't trailing all the way out there again. In any case, Anita had asked him round to Auntie Margaret's on Friday. The Hunchback was going to be there, and a school friend of Anita's called Laurel Davies.

'Feel like coming?' said Pauline.

'Can't.' He shook his head. 'Already going somewhere else.'

'Oh,' she said. 'That's a pity.'

He was inclined to agree with her. Not that he felt any great urge to go to a party at Collier's Wood with a girl who had hang-ups about naked men, but on the whole he felt even less of an urge to go round to Auntie Margaret's and meet the Hunchback and Laurel Davies. He couldn't imagine why Anita had wanted him to. He would have got out of it if he could but she had caught him unawares, turning up in the basement at Plumber's, of all unlikely places — where her appearance had gained him new respect amongst his fellow troglodytes.

'Tasty-looking dish,' had said Dennis, ogling up the basement steps whence Anita had taken her departure.

'Nice bit o' crumpet,' had agreed Big Mac.

'Bit o' crumpet?' Charlie had echoed him scathingly. 'That bird ain't crumpet, you ignorant lout, that bird's class. Definite class.' He'd turned, knowledgably, to Jamie. 'You was quite right about King's Cross, mate . . . I don't reckon she'd have gone for it. Not her style at all.'

He was glad Anita was approved of, but he really couldn't say that he was looking forward to Friday with any kind of eagerness. In fact, when it arrived, it turned out to be every bit as dire as he'd known it would be. A further term of reading history books had done nothing to improve the Hunchback — it had, if anything, made him even worse, even more condescending than he'd been before. He'd now acquired a video cassette machine, and they all had to sit in his sitting room — *his* sitting room — and watch some terribly clever French movie he'd recorded specially off the television to impress them with the night before. As it turned out, Laurel Davies, who was going to university herself in September, happened to speak fluent French, which just at first Jamie hoped might take the wind out of the Hunchback's sails, but no such luck, because naturally the Hunchback also spoke fluent French: they spent the evening ostentatiously speaking it together and sneering at the subtitles.

The obnoxious Babs looked in at one point and

said, 'Oh, are you watching the Jeanne Moreau? Can I stay and see it?'

'No, you can't,' said the Hunchback. 'It's not fit for juveniles.'

'But I'll be *twelve* next year.'

'Sorry: should have said infants. Not fit for infants.'

'*Pas devant*,' said Laurel Davies.

'*Pas devant*,' agreed the Hunchback.

'Why not?' said Babs, greedily feasting her eyes on the screen, where a naked man was in process of climbing out of a bed containing a naked woman.

'Yeah, why not?' said Jamie. 'She's already read *Lady Chatterley*, and she knows all about bum bandits.' (Anita turned to look at him, wide-eyed: Laurel Davies gave a smothered snort of laughter.) 'I don't see how a bit of sub-titled sex can hurt her.'

'That's *right*,' said Babs.

'Done the Kama Sutra yet, have you?' said Jamie.

'Calmer what?'

'Kama Sutra . . . good book. You ought to try it.'

'I will,' said Babs.

'You bloody well won't!' said the Hunchback. He leapt from his seat and propelled the child by one ear from the room, glaring at Jamie as he did so. 'I don't think that was very funny,' he said, as he came back.

'I thought it was hilarious,' said Laurel Davies. 'Has she really read *Lady Chatterley*?'

141

'Of course she hasn't!' snapped the Hunchback. 'And if I find she's gone and got hold of a copy of the Kama Sutra from somewhere —'

'You'll nick it off her,' said Jamie, 'and read it yourself.'

Anita and Laurel both giggled. The Hunchback looked at him with loathing, and later on made a feeble attempt to get his own back.

'And how are you getting on with your ballet dancing?' he said.

Jamie said that he was getting on all right, thank you.

'As a matter of fact, he's doing very well,' said Anita.

He knew she was only trying to be supportive, but he could have wished she hadn't said it. It made him feel about five years old. The Hunchback gave one of his supercilious smiles, top lip curled back showing all his teeth.

'At least you can't complain of a shortage of women.'

'No,' said Jamie. 'I'm not complaining.'

'He hardly could,' said Anita, 'considering he's been out with just about every girl in his class.'

This time, he wasn't so sure that she *was* trying to be supportive, there had been a definite edge to her voice. Later, as she came downstairs to see him off, he found out why.

'You weren't really engaged to that awful Doreen girl, were you?' she said.

He gritted his teeth. (He could have wished he were gritting them on Doreen. She deserved to have a few teeth gritted on her.)

142

''Course I wasn't,' he said.

Anita seemed doubtful.

'She's going round telling everyone that you were.'

'That's because she's mad at me. She's just doing it to get even.'

'But she's showing everyone the ring!'

That rattled him. Don't say she'd gone and picked it up again off the floor of the lift? He wouldn't put it past her.

'What ring?' he said.

'A silver one,' said Anita. 'Quite nice, actually . . . it looks like a wedding ring.'

Relief.

'Well, I've never seen it,' he said. 'If she says I bought it for her then she's making it up.'

'She must be barmy or something,' said Anita.

'Yeah,' said Jamie. 'I reckon she is.'

He'd more or less made up his mind, after the fiasco with Doreen, that he was going to give girls a miss for a bit: his conversation with Anita decided him. He'd done his best, and all he seemed to have proved was that the female of the species was either stark mad or riddled with hang-ups. He couldn't afford to keep *on* getting engaged by mistake — or, come to that, keep on booking hotel rooms and losing his deposit. He decided that as soon as he could scrape together the necessary train fare he would go back home and fetch his Chinese trumpet and devote all his weekends to learning how to play it. From now on, the female seventy-five per cent of Kendra

Hall could get by without him. He'd given them ample opportunity: if they'd failed to take it, then that was their loss. As far as he was concerned, he was through.

He had reckoned without Natalie. On Saturday morning, owing to Pauline being off sick with a twisted ankle (or more likely a hangover from her party), he had her all to himself.

'You're pretty good, aren't you?' she said. 'Doreen was always going on about how good you were. I used to think it was because she had this thing about you.'

'*Doreen* did?'

'Oh, yes! She was crazy over you. Of course, she isn't any more — not after you jilting her like that.'

He thought he detected a note of censure in her voice, but when he looked at her he found that she was laughing.

'It's all right,' she said, 'nobody believes it . . . or if they do, they think she probably only got what she asked for. Daft cow.'

He felt slightly uncomfortable about that. To tell the truth, he wasn't *totally* easy in his conscience where Doreen was concerned. For all it had been a genuine misunderstanding, he wouldn't like to think that she'd really suffered because of it.

'She's a bit of a fantasist,' said Natalie, 'if you ask me.'

He reckoned she was right. That was Doreen's trouble: she was a fantasist. An *arch* fantasist. Getting the OBE, for heaven's sake!

'You doing anything tonight?' said Natalie.

She said it quite casually, as she was preparing to pose en arabesque. He was so surprised he nearly took his arm away and let her go walloping to the ground.

'I thought, if you weren't,' she continued, still just as casual as before (she obviously didn't realize how close she'd come to crashing floorwards) 'you might like to drop round to our place for a meal.'

It wasn't the sort of invitation that anyone in his right senses would refuse. He forgot about giving girls a miss, he forgot about learning to play his Chinese trumpet. Suddenly, there was but one thought in his mind: he was going to make it with Natalie. He didn't care if she did do it all the time, practically with anyone; the fact remained she hadn't yet done it with anyone from the boys' ballet class. He knew she hadn't, because Steven was the only one she'd been out with, and Steven himself had freely admitted that he hadn't taken advantage of the situation.

'Too easy,' he'd said, when Jamie had questioned him about it. 'I like to have to fight for my women.'

Steven could fight if he wished; for his part, Jamie was sick and tired of doing so. If someone were willing to hand it to him on a plate, he reckoned he'd reached the stage where he was prepared to take it. He reckoned he'd earned it. He even felt a bit flattered, in a way. Up until now, if he was to be honest, Natalie hadn't really paid all that much attention to him; Brett and Steven had been her main targets. Brett she had given up as a bad job quite early on, though she'd persisted with Steven for some time, and then, as far as Jamie could make out, it had been Steven who had been the one to call a halt. He laughed when he heard where Jamie was going.

'Into the lions' den . . . sooner you than me!'

Natalie shared a flat (large and sprawling: top floor of old house, Earl's Court) with three other girls, whom she introduced en masse as 'Tricia Lyn 'n Angie'. He never did discover which was which. One of them was big and rather bosomy, one was thin and studious-looking with jet black hair in a pudding basin cut, and the third was a willowy redhead. He was too shy to ask for separate identification, and since, in any case, they were all in ceaseless motion, constantly coming and going, whisking in and out and all over the place, it would have been extremely difficult to keep track even if he had known. Natalie said, 'It's all right, they'll be going out soon,' and sat him down on a sagging sofa in front of a colour television set which nobody was watching.

'Have a lager,' she said. She handed him a can. 'I'll just go and take a look at the food.'

He sat on the sagging sofa, in front of the colour television, drinking his lager straight from the can since she hadn't given him any glass. Every few minutes Tricia Lyn or Angie would appear, in a state of undress, and either snatch something up or throw a few cushions around and say *'Christ!'* in tones of exasperation, then stalk off again. Jamie did his best to keep his eyes fixed on the colour television. The sight of so much naked female flesh was rather disturbing; embarrassing, more than anything. The entire flat seemed to be full of scantily-clad buttocks, all treading a path through the sitting room. There were black silk buttocks, red satin buttocks, and one set where you had to look twice to see that they were clad in anything at all. Natalie came in and sat beside him on the sagging sofa and said again: 'It's all right, they'll be going out soon. I hope you like things hot, by the way . . . I think I've rather overdone it with the chilli.'

The chilli, when at last it materialized (round about nine o'clock) nearly took the roof off his mouth, but since Natalie ate it with every sign of enjoyment, her only comment being that it was 'warmish', he had to assume that either his soft palate was softer than other people's or else he was missing a protective layer of asbestos. The only way he could get through it was by washing down each mouthful with a liberal draught of lager. From time to time Tricia Lyn 'n Angie drifted in and out: they were still half naked.

'It's all right,' said Natalie. 'They'll be going out soon. Let's go and sit on the sofa.'

Sitting on the sofa with Natalie was quite an experience. Unfortunately, being all filled up as he was with lager and burning hot chilli beans, he couldn't concentrate on it absolutely as whole-heartedly as he would have liked; also, the frequent driftings in and out of naked women didn't help.

'Don't let them bother you,' murmured

147

Natalie. 'They'll be going out any minute now.'

After a bit, the willowy redhead appeared (fully clad) and said, 'All clear — I'm on my way.'

'Wonderful,' breathed Natalie. She removed her hand from inside Jamie's sweat shirt. 'Let's decamp . . .'

'Could you just tell me first,' he said, 'where the bathroom is?'

'Second on the left — and don't be all day, because I don't feel like waiting.'

Natalie peeled off into her bedroom: Jamie made a dash for the second door on the left. To his horror and confusion, there was a naked female in there, sitting in the bath. It was the thin, studious-looking one with the pudding basin hair cut. He rather fancied she was Tricia, but he couldn't be certain. Red-faced, he mumbled an apology and started to back out. Tricia (if it was Tricia) flapped a wet hand over the side of the bath and said, 'That's OK, we never lock the door. Just carry on.'

He tried, but nothing would come; not even though five seconds ago he'd been bursting. (And in five seconds' time would be bursting again.) He felt a flush of desperation. How was he supposed to do anything with a naked female sitting watching him? It was impossible; nobody could. He bet even Steven couldn't. The worst of it was, she would *hear* he wasn't doing anything.

No, it wasn't: the worst of it was that Natalie was expecting him to go back and perform, and how could he do *that* when his whole inside was awash with lager?

148

If only she would run the taps, or something. It might bring it on; running water sometimes did.

Needless to say, she didn't run the taps. Just splished and sploshed a bit and idly soaped her rakelike body with a sponge.

In a panic, he pulled the chain, did himself up, and scudded out again into the passage. Which way was the kitchen? There might at least be an empty milk bottle . . .

There probably was an empty milk bottle, but there was also the big bosomy girl, standing in the middle of the floor eating chilli beans in her bra and pants (red silk).

'Sorry!' said Jamie. He shot out again. 'Wrong room!'

Natalie was already undressed and in bed.

'What *have* you been up to?' she said. 'I began to think you'd run off.'

He wished he had the sort of aplomb that could get away with saying, 'I found this naked bird in the bathroom . . . just stopped off to give her a portion.' He bet Steven would have done. He bet, now he came to think of it, that Steven would have peed quite happily in front of her. *He* wouldn't come slinking back with a bladder full to bursting point. It was only idiots like Jamie that got themselves into that sort of situation.

'Come on, then!' Natalie pulled back the edge of the bedclothes and patted the bed. 'Now that you *are* here . . .'

Awkwardly, he stripped off and climbed in beside her. This was the thing he had been working towards — the thing he had dedicated his life

149

to. (Well, as a short-term objective.) It was the thing he had determined to do before the year was out. He had tried it on with Sharon, who had slapped his face; and Pauline, who hadn't liked naked men; and Kate, who couldn't make up her mind; and Doreen, who'd wanted him to marry her: all of them without success. Now there was Natalie; sexy Natalie. And *she* was actually *offering* it him.

There was only one small problem: he couldn't do it. Not with all that lager swilling round inside him. It was no good; he would have to go.

'Boy,' said Natalie, 'have you got a weak bladder!'

He pulled on his jeans and charged off again, bare-chested, to the bathroom. This time, he didn't care if there *was* anyone in there.

This time, there wasn't. He was about half way through when the big bosomy girl walked in. She didn't apologize, or anything; just said 'Hi' in a vague and vacant fashion and turned on the bath taps. He waited for her to go away. Instead, she perched on the edge of the bath and looked at him.

'You at Natalie's ballet school?'

'Yes,' he said; and forced himself to carry on.

The girl yawned.

'I was at ballet school once. Got too fat. I'm in a travel agent's now.'

Jamie said 'Mm?' in what he hoped was a suitably careless tone of voice. (What was the *matter* with these women? Had they never heard of privacy, for goodness' sake?)

'It's not too bad, I suppose,' said the girl. 'Gets a bit of a bore at times — but then, of course, there's all the free travel. I take it you're going to be a dancer?' She studied him, critically. 'You look like a dancer.'

How could she tell whether or not he looked like a dancer? She was only looking at one small bit of him (not that it was as small as all that). Honestly, the place was full of nymphomaniacs. He bet they'd all like to have a go.

He finished off and fled back, considerably relieved, to the bedroom — only to find that in his absence the girl with the pudding basin hair had arrived. She was standing in front of the dressing table, in a dress that seemed to be only half there, looking at herself sideways.

'To wear — or not to wear?'

'To wear,' said Natalie.

'What do you think?' She addressed Jamie through the mirror. 'If you were going out with me . . . would it turn you on, or would it turn you off?'

'Dunno,' he said. The only thing *he* knew was that right at this moment it was turning him off. Right off.

Natalie patted the bed. Selfconsciously, he removed his jeans and scrambled back in.

'It all depends,' said Natalie, 'which one you're going with. If it's the one with the hairy bum —'

'No, it's not. It's the little randy sod.'

'Oh. *Him.*'

'Yes,' said Pudding Basin. '*Him.*'

'I see. Well, that's different.'

'Last time I went anywhere with him —'

Jamie lay and listened, in growing disbelief, as with graphic detail Pudding Basin described what had happened on the last occasion she had gone anywhere with the little randy sod. He could hardly believe it. He hadn't known girls talked like that. (And she looked such a *studious* sort of girl.) Some of the things she said made his hair stand on end. Unfortunately, his hair was the only thing that did.

'Really,' said Natalie, when at last the Pudding Basin had removed herself, 'you're very easily put off, aren't you? Now we shall have to start all over again . . .'

They did so. It was hardly his fault that at the crucial moment there was a bang at the door and the Pudding Basin called out that she was 'Off now . . . see you tomorrow!'

The result was disastrous.

Not only disastrous: catastrophic.

'For goodness' sake!' said Natalie. 'Don't you have *any* control?'

She didn't say it unpleasantly, but he could tell she wasn't pleased.

8

On Monday night, in the canteen, Jamie overheard Natalie talking to Bettina, the black girl
whom he had once fancied but who was now very
firmly the property of Errol.

'The trouble with the ballet,' she was saying,
'is that you can never seem to find a real *man*.'

Steven, standing beside Jamie in the queue,
obviously also overheard. He looked round at
Jamie, in mock reproof.

'And what did *you* do to upset her? Or
perhaps —' he grinned — 'I should say, what
didn't you do?'

Jamie muttered; not amused.

'Cheer up!' said Steven. 'We're both tarred
with the same brush . . . nothing to be ashamed
of.' He raised his voice slightly. 'Take an entire
regiment to satisfy that one.'

Natalie looked back at him, over her shoulder.
She smiled, sweetly.

'I *could* say the same for you.'

'But of course you wouldn't,' said Steven,
'because it wouldn't be nice. Would it?'

Natalie picked up her tray.

'The truth,' she observed, 'quite frequently isn't.'

She stalked off, with Bettina.

'Bitch,' said Steven.

'Belt up! You asked for it.' Jamie pushed him out of the way and reached across, with an air of disgruntlement, for a plate. His performance on Saturday evening had scarcely done very much for his self-esteem, and Steven's attitude, just at this moment, was not helping. He could do without all the silly jokes and innuendo. 'If you sling a bucketful,' he said, 'you're going to get a bucketful slung back. What d'you expect? She's going to take it lying down?'

'Why not? It's the way she takes everything else,' murmured Steven.

'Put a sock in it!' Jamie, losing patience, gave him a shove. Steven twitched an eyebrow.

'Bit touchy,' he said, 'aren't we?'

Friday evening, Jamie stayed indoors — the first Friday he had done so for several weeks. Steven, coming home at ten o'clock, seemed surprised to find him there.

'Not out on the razzle?'

'Does it look like it?' said Jamie. He still hadn't fully recovered from his disgruntlement. He was down to eating toast and Golden Syrup every day, supplemented by the occasional cup of coffee in the canteen at Plumber's or at Kendra Hall and it was doing nothing for his sense of humour.

'What's the problem?' Steven eyed him sympathetically as he lay sprawled in unwashed apathy on a bed that hadn't been made since the last change of sheets, over a fortnight ago. Semi-starvation and a sense of failure hung heavily upon him. He was obviously some kind of sexual inadequate; he had to be, to have screwed it up with Natalie. How was he going to face her in the pas de deux class tomorrow? — how was he going to face any of them in the pas de deux class tomorrow? She was bound to have splashed it about, girls always did. It would be common property by now. When he thought of the conversation that had taken place between her and the Pudding Basin —

'You don't want to let it worry you, you know,' said Steven.

Jamie narrowed his eyes, automatically suspicious.

'Don't want to let what worry me?'

'Whatever went wrong between you and Natalie. I tell you, that girl's a man-eater. She gets through men like other people get through chocolate bars. She'd have put the frighteners on Casanova, never mind you.'

His pride didn't like that. He raised himself on one elbow, thrusting his hair back out of his eyes.

'She didn't put the frighteners on me. I just didn't fancy her.' Oh, you lousy filthy stinking liar, James Carr. 'Like you said —' he rolled over on to his back, placed his hands behind his head — 'she's too easy.' (And may you be forgiven.)

Steven smiled.

'Poor old Natalie! Must be losing her touch. First me, then you . . . nothing but one disappointment after another. She ought to try Percy. He'd give her what she wanted — and some.'

'Percy?' Jamie was sceptical. 'You must be joking!'

Steven shook his head.

'Don't let looks deceive you . . . dead straight, our Percy.'

'How do you know?'

'How do you think I know?'

Jamie hunched a shoulder. He hadn't the faintest idea how Steven knew; and neither, at that moment, did he very much care. He let his head fall back on the lumpy pillow. The ceiling above him was yellowing and flaky. It had jagged tramline cracks running from corner to corner and grimy grey cobwebs floating in strings from the picture rail. If Steven were right, then so much for Pauline and her penetrating insights. *D'you know who the nicest boy is? The nicest one of all? It's Percy. He's sweet; he really is. I wouldn't mind going out with Percy. I'd feel safe with Percy* . . . She'd be in for a shock — *if* Steven were right.

He rolled over again, on to his side.

'You sure about Percy?'

'My son, I don't make mistakes about things like that . . . can't afford to.'

'What d'you mean, you can't afford to?'

'Can't afford the waste of time. Unlike Natalie, this boy doesn't believe in proceeding by trial and error.'

Jamie looked at him. Uncertain; suddenly wary.

'Not only that —' Steven seated himself, thoughtfully, on the edge of the bed — 'one doesn't care for rejection. A bit of a fight is one thing; but an outright slap in the face —' He was watching Jamie as he spoke. Jamie arched away slightly. 'Rejection,' said Steven, 'is bad for the soul. Which is why, had I been Natalie, I wouldn't have touched me with a barge pole — and why, contrariwise, being me, I wouldn't lay even the discreetest of fingers on our Percy. Much as I might like to. He may give the impression of being a nice little number, but believe you me —' He broke off. 'What's the matter?'

'Nothing.' Jamie swung his legs over the side of the bed and sat up. 'Nothing's the matter.'

'Then why are you sitting there looking like some outraged virgin?'

He could hardly say that he wasn't sitting there looking like some outraged virgin. If that was the way he came across, then that was the way he came across — and maybe it wasn't so far from the truth, at that. Maybe he did feel a certain sense of outrage. If not outrage, at any rate grievance. All that guff Steven had given him way back at the beginning — *The whole business is lousy with flaming poufdahs*. Those were his exact words; Jamie could still hear him saying them. *The whole business is lousy with flaming poufdahs. Look at that old Winston Woo . . . a right little raver*. Talk about a cover-up job! He'd got every right to feel aggrieved. If people couldn't even have the courage of their own convictions —

'I take it,' said Steven, 'that you had twigged? About me? I mean . . . it's not exactly news?'

Looking back on it, he could see that he probably *ought* to have twigged; but the fact was, he hadn't.

'If you mean,' he said coldly (he couldn't help the cold bit: it was caused by embarrassment. What mainly embarrassed him was his own naïveté), 'if you mean did I know you wanted to screw Percy, then no, I didn't.'

'Oh, now, come on!' Steven laughed. 'Don't go all po-faced and moral majority on me.'

'I'm not going all po-faced and moral majority!' He resented that. Just because he was a bit slow on the uptake, that didn't mean he was any tight-lipped prude. 'I don't give a damn who you want to screw.'

'So long as I don't try it on you?'

'Yeah. Well —' (why should he feel he had to apologize?) — 'it's just not a scene I happen to go for.'

'How do you know?' said Steven. 'Ever tried it?'

'No,' said Jamie. 'Never tried chicken-molesting, either.'

'Really? You amaze me! I thought every red-blooded male above the age of puberty had had a go at chickens. Allow me to say, my son, that you don't know what you're missing.'

'Some things,' said Jamie, 'I don't mind missing.'

'You mean to tell me you have no natural curiosity?'

'Only in certain directions.'

'And this isn't one of them?'

This most certainly wa̲s̲ ̲ bed
Steven leaned towards him.

'How can you be so sure?'

'It's just one of those things —' prudently, Jamie removed himself from the bed — 'that I feel. Instinctively. Like with chickens . . . I feel, instinctively, inside myself, that molesting a chicken wouldn't do a thing for me.'

'Well, all right, you don't have to pick up your skirts and go running off in a panic . . . I'm not going to rape you.'

That made him laugh. Steven regarded him quizzically.

'What's so funny? You think I couldn't?'

'I'd like to see you try!'

'Why?' Steven lay back on the bed, contemplating him through half-closed eyes. 'What would you do if I did? Scream for help like some suburban spinster?'

'You'd be the one screaming for help,' said Jamie, 'not me.'

A slow grin spread itself across Steven's face.

'I might scream . . . but I very much doubt if it would be for help!'

'Well, whatever it would be for,' said Jamie, 'I don't advise trying it.'

'Oh, you don't have to worry! I'm not into sado-masochism. But I could seduce you, my son, if I really put my mind to it. Make no mistake about that.'

Jamie looked at him.

'You reckon?'

'I reckon.' Steven suddenly sprang up, off the

You. Come down the boozer and I'll stand you a pint . . . well, come on!' He jerked his head, impatient, at the door. 'You're quite safe down there. I'm not going to seduce you in front of half Hammersmith, am I?'

'Not going to seduce me anywhere,' said Jamie. That wasn't the reason he was hesitating; he could cope with that. The reason he was hesitating was in case he got thrown out. He glanced at his reflection in the flyblown mirror above the Victorian mantelshelf. Was it his imagination or was he looking older?

It was not his imagination: he was, quite definitely, looking older. His cheeks were all sunken, and he had bags under his eyes. There was also a faint but discernible shadow round the line of his jaw. The experience of the past few weeks, he thought, had aged him.

'So are you coming,' said Steven, 'or aren't you?'

'Yeah, OK.' He grabbed his jacket off the back of a chair. 'I'm coming.'

Three pints of beer (he was not thrown out) in quick succession were three more than he was used to. They did not make him drunk — not what you would call *drunk* — but they did induce a certain unsteadiness of balance when climbing up stairs.

'For crying out loud!' Steven hooked an arm through Jamie's, binding him tightly to his side. Jamie looked at him, owlishly.

'Is this all part of some dire-bolcal plot?'

'Don't be an arseole,' said Steven. He said it quite amiably. 'What use do you think you'd be to anyone in this state?'

He didn't remember taking his clothes off and getting into bed, but obviously he must have done because when he woke up — some time in the middle of the night if the darkness and the silence were anything to go by — he was unmistakably in bed and unmistakably minus his clothes. He didn't seem to have bothered putting his pyjamas on; they must, presumably, still be under the pillow. He put up a hand to feel for them, and as he did so felt something else. Something that ought not to have been there. It felt like human flesh — it was human flesh. He shot up the bed.

'What the bloody hell are you playing at?'

'What the bloody hell are you?' retorted Steven. 'That was my eye you nearly gouged out.'

'Well, what the hell is your eye doing on my pillow?'

'Just resting there ... I happened,' said Steven, 'to be asleep.'

'Yeah? Well, this happens,' said Jamie, 'to be my bed ... go on!' He gave him a kick. 'Shove off, and stop buggering about.'

'I'm not buggering about! I wouldn't dream of taking advantage of someone when they're non compos mentis ... it may interest you to know that you have been snoring like a sty full of prize porkers. I've had to keep turning you over.'

'I'll flaming well turn you over,' said Jamie, 'if you don't shove off.'

161

'Have a heart! My bed's freezing cold.'

'That's your problem.'

'Jamie . . .' Steven put up a hand and coaxingly caressed Jamie's cheek: Jamie swatted at it, crossly.

'Look, I told you already . . . I'm not into that scene. I thought you said you didn't like rejection?'

'I don't.'

'Well, then! Why ask for it?'

Steven made a little whimpering noise.

'You don't know what it's like, wanting someone and not being able to have them.'

Oh, don't I? thought Jamie. He reflected, rather sourly, on all the women that he had wanted and not been able to have. Sharon, Pauline, Kate — Anita. Steven should tell *him* he didn't know what it was like?

'It's been torture,' said Steven, 'these last few weeks. You don't know how badly I've wanted you.'

So what was he supposed to be? Flattered?

'At least with Pauline and Kate you were free to ask them. The worst you could get was your face slapped. How do you think I've been feeling? Knowing if I even so much as hinted at it I'd run the risk of having you walk out on me?'

Jamie gave him another shove.

'You should've thought of that before.'

'Before what?'

'Before suggesting I move in with you.'

'How could I? *I* didn't know I was going to start feeling like this. You can't regulate the way you're going to start feeling about someone. It's something that just happens.' -

'So you should've taken it into account.'

Steven looked at him, reproachfully. He could hear from the tone of his voice that it was reproachful.

'Don't be so censorious.'

'I'm not being censorious! I'm just saying you should have taken it into account.'

'Well, I didn't. All right, so I made a fundamental error. It's easy enough for you to talk.'

'No, it's not,' said Jamie.

'Yes, it is! You don't know what it's like —'

'I do flaming know what it's like!'

'Then why won't you let me?' said Steven.

'Because I told you . . . it's not my scene.'

'What does that matter? Taking flowers to little old ladies probably isn't your scene, but I bet if your old granny were in hospital you'd go and take her flowers quickly enough; wouldn't you?'

Jamie frowned.

'There does happen to be a slight difference.'

'Dead right there happens to be a slight difference! The slight difference is that when it comes to making your grandmother happy you care, and when it comes to making me happy you don't. That's what you actually mean when you keep parroting that it isn't your scene. You know that it would bring *me* great happiness, but just because you don't anticipate getting anything out of it yourself, not *even* from making me happy, as you would with your grandmother, although as a matter of fact you're quite wrong, and I'll guarantee to *prove* to you that you're wrong if only you'll give me half a chance, but just because you mistakenly *think* that you won't get anything out of it and don't happen to care two straws about whether I will or not, you have to go and rationalize and say it's not your scene. You wouldn't tell your grandmother that it wasn't your scene, would you? Of course you wouldn't! You'd go galloping off with a big bunch of roses as fast as your legs would carry you, just for the pleasure of making her happy; and I really don't see,' said Steven, growing maudlin, 'I really don't see why I shouldn't be just as entitled as your grandmother to my share of life's happiness. Anyone would think I was making unspeakable demands. All I'm asking for is a bit of love.'

'All you're asking for,' said Jamie, sternly, 'is a bit of sex.'

'So what's wrong with that?'

Just for a moment, he was stumped for an answer.

'I put it to you,' said Steven, 'when set beside people blowing people up, and people inventing things to torture people with, and people burning food that other people could eat, and other people making neutron bombs that could tear the entire world apart so that there wouldn't be any more people left, not ever, *any*where . . . what is wrong with me asking you for something that isn't going to do any conceivable harm to a single living soul?'

Nothing, thought Jamie; there wasn't anything wrong with it.

'If you invented a bomb,' said Steven, 'and it was a really good bomb that would really kill millions of people all at one fell swoop, they'd probably give you a medal. They'd rationalize, of course; they have to do that, or they'd go mad. What they say is that making these really good bombs that can really kill millions of people all at one go is actually in the long run saving lives. If they didn't say that, they couldn't stand it. That's the morality we live by — and I say it stinks. Do you agree, or don't you?'

'Yeah.' Jamie nodded: he agreed.

'So what's all the argument about? All this crap about *it's not my scene? — what's* not your scene? You want medals? You want their bits of tin saying you've been a good boy and played their false morality games? You want their *approval*? Is that what you want?'

'I never said I wanted their approval.'

'So why are you being all mean and prissy?'

That was too much; that was more than he could take. He hadn't accused Pauline or Kate of being mean or prissy, and he didn't see why he should be accused of being so.

'I think I ought to tell you,' he said, 'that I'm getting really bored with this conversation.'

'Then why go on with it? Why not just give in and say yes? I don't see what's stopping you.'

'The same thing that's stopping me saying practically anything at all . . . you, principally.'

'What do you mean, me principally?'

'Flaming talking all the time.'

'So I'm pleading my cause!'

'So you're like a mouth on a flaming stick. Why you can't just shut up —'

'And put the action where my mouth is?'

And get back to your own bed, was what he had actually been going to say.

'Do you realize,' said Steven, 'that someone could have their finger on the button right at this very minute and we could all of us end up dead?'

'That is very true,' said Jamie. 'And that being the case I am asking you, for the last time, to kindly remove your great carcase from my sleeping patch so that I can at least have the benefit of a good night's rest before it happens.'

Steven made a noise of disgust.

'Some people,' he said, 'are just so trivial it's pathetic.'

Next morning, when Jamie woke up, he was relieved to find that he had his bed to himself. He lay for a few minutes, staring up at the cracks in the ceiling and wondering how he felt. On the whole, he decided, he didn't feel anything very much. Certainly he wasn't going to nurse any grudges, if Steven wasn't. Not that he could see any reason why Steven should. He, after all, had borne no grudges against Kate or Pauline — well, perhaps just passing grudges. Nothing lasting. He had always accepted it as their right to say no. Provided Steven played the game according to the same rules there wasn't any reason, as far as he was concerned, why they should have to fall out, or even part company if it came to that. He didn't hold it against the guy for trying: just so long as he didn't *persist*.

The door opened and Steven came in.

'Hi.'

Jamie sat up.

'Where've you been?'

'Downstairs; get the post . . . here!' He tossed an envelope on to the bed. 'See how that grabs you.'

Jamie picked it up. His stomach promptly performed a double somersault. In a neat little box in the left-hand corner of the envelope was a picture of a Victorian mansion surrounded by trees: beneath it, the words *Kendra Hall*.

'Well, go on!' said Steven. 'Open it!'

Jamie moistened his lips.

'You opened yours?'

'Yup.'

'What did it —'

'Offered me a place for September . . . look, if I've got through the damned thing I'm bloody sure you have. Stop pratting about and get that envelope undone.'

He swallowed. He hadn't realized, until this moment, just how much it meant to him — how much depended on it. All the difference between achievement and non-achievement: between a lifetime at Plumber's and —

'For God's sake!' Steven snatched the envelope away from him. 'If you're not going to do it, then let me . . . there you are, you great berk!' He thrust a sheet of paper under Jamie's nose. 'What did I tell you?'

'I'm in?'

'Of course you're flaming well in! If anyone was going to get through, you were.'

Relief washed over him in a great, debilitating wave. The number of times he had laughed at Anita — got mad at Anita — lectured her for taking things too seriously, for attaching too much importance —

'Do I get a reward,' said Steven, 'for being the bearer of such glad tidings?'

'What?' Jamie looked up, abstractedly. 'What's the time?'

'Ten past eight; why?'

He threw back the bedclothes.

'I've got to go to Ealing.'

'At ten past eight?'

'I want to catch Anita before she leaves for home.'

'Telephone her.'

'No.' He wanted to be there, to see her reaction when he gave her the news. It would mean as much to her as it did to him. Firmly, he removed Steven from his path and began collecting up scattered articles of clothing from the floor. Steven watched him a while.

'No hard feelings?' he said, at last.

'What about?'

'Last night.'

'Oh! That.' He shrugged his shoulders. 'Forget it.'

'You mean you're not going to take umbrage and start screaming you want out?'

'I might,' said Jamie, 'if I were as small-minded as you accused me of being.'

Steven grinned.

'For that, I apologize.'

'So you flaming well ought.'

Jamie went across to the wash basin and broke open the communal face flannel. (As a result of not having been used for a day or so it had grown a trifle stiff in its folds.)

'You must admit,' said Steven, 'it was a fair try.'

'Waste of time,' said Jamie. 'I did warn you.'

'Ah, well!' Steven sighed; philosophical. 'You win some, you lose some . . . what are you doing this evening?'

'Nothing; I'm broke.'

'Feel like coming to the cinema?'

'I can't, I told you . . . I've got no bread.'

'So I'll treat you.'

Jamie turned, and looked at him.

'It's all right! Scout's honour — no strings attached, no funny stuff. Strictly a business arrangement. You can do the same for me on pay day.'

'OK,' said Jamie. 'You're on.'

Mrs Archer opened the door to him in Ealing: he caught Anita as she was sitting down to breakfast with Auntie Margaret. Fortunately there were only the two of them. Uncle Richard, as usual, was away on business, the Hunchback was back at his history books, and Babs safely incarcerated in her progressive boarding school in the depths of Surrey.

'Jamie! How nice!' Auntie Margaret looked up

with a smile and invitingly patted the empty chair at her side. She always greeted him as if he were one of the family, which by now, in spite of sunken baths and low-slung coffee tables, not to mention the acres of white carpet, he almost began to feel he was. 'Have you eaten? No? Then come and sit down — Anita, be a pet and run down to the kitchen and ask Mrs A. if she'd mind rustling up some more bacon and eggs. I'm sure Jamie could do with some, couldn't you?'

He certainly wouldn't say no. Bacon and eggs would be the most substantial meal he had eaten since Natalie's super-hot chilli beans.

He didn't tell Anita his news while Auntie Margaret was there. He kept nearly doing so and then at the last minute stopping himself: it was too important to be blurted out over bacon and eggs.

They had reached the toast and marmalade stage before Anita, elaborately casual, said: 'Did you come round for any special reason, or —?'

'Got something to show you.'

'Something to *show* me?' He nodded. She stared at him, her eyes alight with a mixture of eagerness and apprehension. 'About your audition?'

'Could be,' he said.

'Well!' Auntie Margaret laid down her napkin. 'I must be making a beeline, I'm due at the Red Cross in half an hour.' She pushed back her chair. 'I'll leave you two to get on with it.'

The minute Auntie Margaret had gone, Anita stopped eating toast and marmalade and said

170

'Jamie?' He pulled the letter out of the back of his jeans.

'Read this.'

Nervously, she took it from him. Her face had suddenly gone very pale. It was always fairly pale, but not it was even paler than usual. Slowly, she unfolded the letter. He watched her as she read it. He watched the colour come flooding into her cheeks: the warm, bright pinkness of pleasure.

'*Jamie!*' For a moment, he thought she might be going to jump up and come round and fling her arms about him and kiss him, as she had once before, when they had danced together in Miss Tucker's show. Indeed, for a moment he was almost sure that she was going to; but then, at the last second, it seemed as if something held her back. She gave a little laugh — almost embarrassed — and dropped her eyes to her toast and marmalade.

'You frightened me . . . I thought it was going to be bad news.'

'I wouldn't have come if it had been bad news.'

'Wouldn't you?' She raised her eyes; very serious. 'Wouldn't you really?'

'What? After all that junk Thea was giving me? *Of course, YOU'll have had no difficulty —*'

She laughed again; not embarrassed any more.

'Well, you didn't have, did you?'

He grinned.

'Seems not.'

'Have you told your parents?'

'Not yet; haven't had a chance.'

'Or Thea? Oh, Jamie, you must tell Thea! She'll be so pleased.'

'You tell her,' he said.

'No, I can't! You've got to. Why don't you come home this weekend? Then you could go and see her.'

For a moment he was tempted. The prospect of telling Miss Tucker was certainly enticing. He could go up to Tenterden while he was there and see if the Hubbard were around. He sometimes was, on a Saturday afternoon, refereeing soccer matches or supervising the camera club. The Hubbard would be glad to hear he'd made it. And Kim — she'd do her bits and pieces. But it was Miss Tucker he'd most like to tell. She wouldn't make a fuss, because Thea never did. She'd probably just pat him on the head, in th‹t way that she had, and say, 'Good boy. Well done. Of course, I never had any doubts.' That would be all; but it would be enough. The only problem was, he hadn't got the train fare.

'The only problem is,' he said, 'I haven't got the train fare. Not only that,' (as Anita opened her mouth, almost certainly to say that she would *lend* him the train fare), 'I've already kind of gone and arranged to do something else . . . I said I'd go to the cinema with Steven.'

'*Steven*?' said Anita. He had the feeling she wasn't very impressed.

'Yeah. Well —' It was just one of those things. He'd done it now. To change his mind at this stage would look like rejection. 'I could come next week,' he said.

172

'You can't come next week. It's the Gala.'

Her tone was cold and accusing. How could he have forgotten about the Gala? It was the biggest thing in the school calendar. He had known about it for weeks.

'How about the week after?' he said.

'You'll have to have told people by *then*.'

'But I could still come home,' he urged.

'Yes; I suppose so.' She fiddled for a moment with the small silver ring she wore on the little finger of her right hand. 'If you're not doing anything else — next week, I mean — if you're not going to the cinema with Steven . . . would you like to come to a party?'

He hesitated; instinctively cautious.

'Who's giving it?' For all he knew, it could be the Hunchback, having a break from his history books.

'Martin Redshanks — he's just got into the Royal Ballet. Actually, he's the one I'm dancing with. At the Gala. We're doing a pas de deux together.'

'Yeah, I know,' said Jamie. 'You told me.' She'd told him about ten times, which was what made it even more unforgivable that he hadn't remembered.

'It's a sort of celebration,' said Anita. 'Everybody's coming.'

'What, everybody in your class?'

'The whole school . . . everybody.'

'You mean, everybody that's full-time.' There was a sharp dividing line between the full-time and the part-time students. The full-time definitely

173

felt themselves a cut above the latter. 'He wouldn't want any of the rabble there,' said Jamie. 'Not if he's just got into the Royal Ballet.'

'But you're not rabble! Not now.' She said it quite unblushingly. He evidently *had* been rabble, up until about ten minutes ago. 'Why don't you come? Then you could meet them all.'

'I might.' In general he liked the idea of being at a party with Anita, but he wasn't too sure that he liked the idea of being with her at this particular one. She would be surrounded by her cronies from Kendra Hall; he would be the outsider — the gatecrasher, the part-timer. It would put him at a disadvantage, and he was already at quite enough of one where his relationship with Anita was concerned. He didn't fancy adding to it. 'I'll think about it,' he said. 'I'll let you know.' He pushed his plate away, the half-eaten toast still upon it. 'Are you going up to the station?'

He walked up there with her, and waited while she bought her ticket.

'I'll call you,' he said, 'about the party.'

'All right.' She hesitated. 'Are you absolutely certain you can't come home this weekend? I mean . . . just going to the cinema —' She looked at him, rather wistfully. 'Couldn't you get out of it?'

He *could* get out of it; no problem about that. All he had to do was say that he was sorry, something else had turned up, or sorry he couldn't make it. He didn't have to explain — he wasn't under any obligation. Steven didn't own him. Just because he'd *said* he'd go, didn't mean that he *had* to go. Anyone could have a change of heart.

'It's not that I couldn't,' he said, 'it's just that —'

'Don't worry.' Anita stooped, to pick up her bag. 'It's not earth-shattering.'

He called after her, as she disappeared through the barrier: 'I'll give Thea a bell . . . I promise.'

9

Of the boys, Steven, Jamie and Errol had been offered places for September: of the girls, only Doreen. Natalie tossed her head and said she'd already decided not to take up a place even if one had been offered her. Who wanted to spend the next twenty years slogging away at boring ballet exercises? Kate put on a brave face and declared that for her part she was now going to start eating like a pig — jam doughnuts, chocolate dips, peanut butter — all the things she liked best and had been depriving herself of for years. Pauline said that she would try for somewhere else. No one seemed surprised that Doreen had got through.

'She may be an absolutely *stupid* cow,' said Natalie, 'but she can dance.'

Maybe she wasn't such a fantasist after all, reflected Jamie. Maybe one of these days she just might end up with an OBE . . . He tried offering her his congratulations, but she was still too offended with him to speak. He most sincerely hoped that come September he wouldn't find himself stuck with partnering her again.

He was still dithering about whether or not to

attend the party on Saturday evening when the great Redshanks came and sought him out *in person* in the canteen before class.

'Are you coming to my do? Anita said she'd asked you. Do come, if you can — and, of course, any other of your lot who've managed to get through.' But none of the riff raff; *please*. 'It's 64 Dewhurst Gardens . . . just around the corner. Basement flat. Look forward to seeing you.'

On the way home that evening, he put the idea to Steven. Steven was not enthusiastic.

'That load of gawkers? You're not going to go, are you?'

'Dunno.' He still hadn't quite made up his mind. A party, undeniably, was a party — and if he were lucky he might just be able to snatch a few minutes alone with Anita. 'I'll probably look in,' he said. 'See what it's like.'

Steven pulled a face.

'In that case, I suppose I'd better come along.'

'You don't have to.'

'Oh, I might as well — if only to keep an eye on you. Make sure you don't get up to any mischief.'

He grinned, trying to pretend that he was only joking. Jamie shrugged.

'It's up to you. D'you want to tell Doreen about it?'

'Not particularly. Why?'

'Well, it's no good me doing it, she just looks straight through me.'

'Oh, if I must,' said Steven.

Doreen, when applied to, said grandly that she had better things to do than fritter away her time at parties.

'She says,' reported Steven, 'that staying up late saps your energy.'

Just as well, really. If Doreen had been there Anita might have thought he'd gone and got engaged again. He wouldn't want any more misunderstandings of that nature. Errol also declined, on the grounds that he was already going somewhere else — 'Which just leaves the two of us,' said Steven, 'in the camp of the enemy . . . you realize we shall almost certainly be spat upon and generally reviled?'

'We'll survive.'

'You might — I happen to be a very delicate flower. Why don't we change our minds and go out for a meal instead? I'll treat you.'

'No way.' He had already telephoned Anita to confirm that he was going. He couldn't back out now. 'If it's really lousy, we don't have to stay.'

The annual Gala was held on Saturday evening in the school's own theatre. It was an important event, attended by critics from all the big London dailies and people from ballet companies on the look-out for talent.

'Not that you ever get offered anything from a Gala performance,' said Anita. 'Not unless you're one of the star turns.'

Anita, being only in her first year, was not yet a star turn, but Mummy and Daddy were coming in spite of that. He saw them in the foyer, as he and Steven arrived: they were talking to Miss Tucker, and they had Kim with them. (He wondered whose bright idea that had been.) Unwillingly, because you never quite knew with Kim what embarrassments she might call down upon you, he went across with Steven.

'Ah!' said Miss Tucker. 'Another of my successful pupils!'

'*Jamie*! Isn't it *won*derful? Aren't you *clever*?' Kim hurled herself at him, joyously. 'This time next year we'll be coming to see *you*!'

He wouldn't have minded her saying it; it was just that she said it in a voice loud enough for the entire assembled company to hear. Sternly, he disentangled himself.

'Who brought you along?'

'Anita's parents — in their *car*.'

'Fancy a lift back?' That was Daddy, offering him the lure of the XJS.

'He's not coming back,' said Kim. She looked at Jamie, accusingly. 'He *never* comes back. He stays up in London and does things by himself — *and* he never tells us what they are.'

He knew from that that his mother must have been speculating. He could just see her, sitting there in the evenings with Kim, while the old man was downstairs selling booze.

'I wonder what he gets up to? I hope he's not keeping bad company. I've said all along he's too young — he's too easily influenced. That boy he's sharing with . . .'

He caught Steven's eye, and wondered what the fool was grinning at.

'Tonight, as it happens —' he addressed himself pointedly to Kim — 'I'm going to a party. Is that all right with your Highness?'

She pouted.

'What about last week? *And* the week before? *And* the —'

'Be fair,' said Steven. 'He has to be let off the lead sometimes.'

Kim looked at him with cold distaste. Steven winked at her, and she turned away, with an air of haughtiness that ill became her button nose.

'Look,' said Jamie, 'I'll be back next weekend. How about that?'

She wavered.

'Is it a promise?'

'Cut my throat if I tell a lie.'

'Let's hold him to it,' said Mummy. 'Let's issue him with a formal invitation ... why don't you come and have lunch with us next Sunday, Jamie?'

Confused, he mumbled that he would like that very much.

'There you are!' Mummy turned, triumphant, to Kim. 'That's got him for you. He can't very well back out of that.'

'He'd better *not*,' said Kim.

Fortunately, since students from the school were expected to wait until the rest of the audience had found seats and then to scatter themselves amongst any that were left, he did not have to suffer the agony of actually sitting next to her — or, indeed, of being anywhere near her, since for the Gala performance all seats were taken and they had to stand, at the back.

In the first half of the programme Anita was merely one of the corps, but after the interval she was given the peasant pas de deux from Act I of *Giselle*: the person she danced it with was Martin Redshanks.

'Flaming gawker,' said Steven.

It was his latest term of abuse. Jamie wasn't absolutely certain what it was supposed to mean, but if it meant what he thought it meant then he concurred: totally and utterly. There was something about Mr Redshanks that really needled him. Maybe it was his hair, sleek and blond and beautiful, with never a strand out of place; or maybe it was his profile, which looked as if it had been carved with geometrical precision from a block of marble — or maybe, more basely, it was the simple fact that he was dancing with Anita. Whatever it was, the guy was a pain.

'I told you,' said Steven, 'he's a gawker.' After a moment's reflection, he added: 'Of the Fifth Dan.'

The gawker of the Fifth Dan shared his basement with two other boys, both of them students at Kendra Hall. By the time Jamie and Steven arrived (having stopped off at a nearby pub for a quick pint and to pick up a couple of bottles) the party was already under way, even though the Gawker himself had not yet put in an appearance: neither, as Jamie quickly observed, had Anita.

He and Steven stood together, by the drinks table, surveying the scene.

'Gawkers,' said Steven. 'The lot of 'em. I knew we shouldn't have come.'

'Well, give it a chance! We've only been here five seconds.'

'That,' said Steven, 'is what's worrying me.'

'I don't know what your gripe is.' Jamie considered a small knot of girls, communing together in a corner. Some of them were quite pretty. 'They're not such a bad lot,' he said, 'on the whole.'

Glumly, Steven followed his gaze.

'If that's the sort of thing that turns you on.'

'It is,' said Jamie. 'Yes.' Let there be no mistake about it: he was definitely girl-oriented. The pity of it was that so few girls seemed to be men-oriented. He sometimes wondered, deep down, if girls really *liked* men, or if they simply looked upon them as a necessary evil.

'Don't look now,' said Steven, 'but your lady friend has just arrived.'

He looked, and saw Anita, flushed and sparkling, in a little white dress that ended half way down her thighs and her hair all about her shoulders. She was hand in hand with the Gawker.

'Angels!' cried the Gawker, to the room in general. 'Lovely to see you all . . . *so* sorry we're late. We were unavoidably detained . . . you understand how it is.'

Laughter broke out. The Gawker looked pleased, Anita embarrassed. She turned, and said something, but the Gawker only winked, in roguish fashion, and shook his head.

'Here,' said Steven. 'Have a drink.'

Jamie took the glass that was being held out to him. He didn't particularly want a drink, but he couldn't just stand there doing nothing. Anita and the Gawker were coming towards them: it would look foolish to be caught doing nothing.

'My dears!' screeched the Gawker. With the flush of performance still upon him, he had grown decidedly shrill. 'Bliss that you could come! Did you like the show?' Without waiting for a reply, he pushed Anita forward. 'Wasn't she wonderful? Wasn't she too utterly divine?'

'Utterly,' said Steven.

'Absolute heaven to partner! — But of course you know all about that, don't you? You've danced with her.'

Jamie risked a quick glance, caught Anita's eye, and hastily looked away again before they could both be embarrassed.

'Don't you think she's heaven?' brayed the Gawker. 'There are some women I could willingly drop from a great height, but you, my precious —' he raised Anita's hand to his lips: Jamie felt a desire to throw up — 'you are not one of them. What'll you drink? What can I get you? Nothing? You're quite sure? Well, you just stay here and talk to Johnny — sorry! Forgive me. Slip of the tongue. Jimmy, isn't it? You just stay here and talk to Jimmy while I go and put some decent music on. Don't run away — I'll be back.'

The Gawker whisked himself off, across the room. He was wearing skin-tight trousers of lightest blue and a pale lemon shirt, frilled at the edges and open to the waist. Jamie hesitated to tar him with the same brush as he had once, mistakenly, tarred Percy. It seemed his judgement in such matters was not all that it might be.

'Well!' said Steven. He wagged an admonitory finger at Anita. 'And where have you been, my pretty maid? I've been a-flirting, sir, she said —'

Anita's blush, which had almost receded, came flooding back in full force.

'Miss Flowerdew was talking to us.'

'Ho hum! A likely tale.'

'She was,' said Anita.

'Of course.' Steven spoke kindly. 'Are you quite certain you won't have a drink? Cool yourself down?'

'Well . . . perhaps just an orange juice.'

'An orange juice —'

Steven turned away to the drinks table.

'We bumped into your parents in the foyer,' said Jamie.

'Did you? Did they —'

'They had the Whizz Kid with them.' That was Steven, over his shoulder. 'The Kimono . . . very cross and angry with Big Brother for being a naughty boy and not reporting home every weekend. A *rather* sticky moment when she wanted to know what he *did*. — *Voilà! Un jus d'orange pour Madame.*'

Anita smiled, uncertainly, as she took the glass.

'Thank you.'

'*Je vous en prie.*'

Steven gave a little bow. Jamie looked at him, irritably. Why couldn't he go away and talk to someone else? Steven was all right by himself, but the minute a third person appeared on the scene he had this habit of taking over.

'Your mother invited me to lunch next Sunday,' said Jamie.

'Did she?' Anita regarded him, anxiously. 'Are you coming?'

'Don't worry.' Steven placed an arm about Jamie's shoulder; casual, but yet proprietorial. 'I'll see he gets there — I wouldn't dare not, after that little lecture the Kimono gave us.'

'She wasn't lecturing *you*,' said Jamie. It had nothing to do with Steven; nothing whatsoever. Firmly, he removed himself from the encirclement of his arm. 'It was me she was having a go at.'

'But it was me she held responsible . . . if looks could kill, I'd be a corpse by now.'

Why couldn't he just belt up? Or go *away*, for God's sake?

'What time shall I come round?' said Jamie.

'Oh . . . one o'clock-ish? Daddy will bring us back afterwards, of course.'

'How super,' said Steven, 'to have a daddy . . . my miserable old skinflint wouldn't give me the pickings from his nose, never mind a lift in his precious motor vehicle.'

'Your miserable old skinflint is probably only miserable,' said Jamie, 'because he's got you for a son. Enough to make anyone miserable.'

Steven turned, mock deprecating, to Anita.

'He doesn't mean a word of it . . . he loves me really.'

'Don't kid yourself.'

'Go on!' Steven winked. 'Give us a kiss and stop being so grumpy.'

'Get knotted,' said Jamie. There were times when Steven could be distinctly trying. He was only doing it to show off, though God knows who

185

he thought he was impressing. Certainly he wasn't impressing Anita. He could tell from the way her nose had gone all pinched that she didn't find him funny. He was on the point of asking her if she felt like dancing, when the Gawker reappeared.

'Sorry, angels, but she is mine . . . I have first claim.' Gaily, he seized Anita by the hand. 'Come!'

With a puzzled little frown at Jamie, she went. Steven picked up Jamie's discarded glass and drained the contents.

'Strange,' he murmured, 'how they always seem to go for the gawkers.'

Certainly it looked as though Anita did. For the rest of the evening he couldn't get near her. Every time he looked up she was dancing with the Gawker, talking with the Gawker, listening to the Gawker, laughing at things the Gawker had said, hanging pink-cheeked and dewy-eyed on every cretinous word that fell from his flabby lips. Just to compound her crime, she was doing it ostentatiously, giggling and flaunting herself in a way he would never have thought her capable of. By half-eleven he had had as much as he could take.

'Shall we depart?' said Steven.

He could see no reason for staying.

'I'll just go and make an announcement.'

'How awfully polite! Why bother?'

Because he wanted to bother. He wanted the chance of just one final word with Anita. She was currently clinging to the Gawker's arm, one of a fond circle of admirers before whom he was holding court. Jamie broke, without ceremony, into their midst.

'Thanks for the party,' he said. 'We'll be off now.'

'My dear!' The Gawker opened wide his blue eyes in astonishment. 'So soon?'

'Yeah. Well —' Jamie looked hard at Anita. She tilted her chin. 'I'll see you next Sunday,' he said. 'About one o'clock.'

'Well,' said Mrs Carr. 'That's nice . . . going to lunch.'

It would be all right, he thought, so long as they didn't have anything too fancy — anything he didn't know how to deal with. He still hadn't altogether recovered from the episode of the artichokes.

'What are you wearing?' His mother fussed about him, busily. 'Something nice? I hate these sweatshirts and jeans all the time. I suppose you live in them up in town — not that it matters up there, there's nobody to see you. But going to lunch at Anita's —' She approved of Anita. Right from the start she'd preferred her to Sharon. 'That Sharon,' as she used to call her. 'Anita always looks smart. She dresses very well.'

'She looked super at the Gala,' said Kim.

'She knows how to wear clothes,' said Mrs Carr. 'What's more, she's got the figure for it. Very trim. She could almost have been a model, with a figure like that.'

'Anita wouldn't want to be a *model*,' said Kim.

'I don't see why not. I'm sure she'd do it very

nicely. She's got the looks, and the education.'

'For crying out loud!' Jamie pushed past his mother and headed impatiently for the door. All this sycophantic eulogising (new words, learnt from Steven: it seemed it was what gawkers did) was more than he could take. He thought as highly of Anita as anyone, but to say that she was educated was simply ludicrous. Get her on any subject other than the ballet and the depths of her ignorance were positively frightening.

'Models are *dumb*,' said Kim. 'And *skinny*.'

'Yeah, well, she'd qualify on that count,' said Jamie. 'Skinny as a flaming broom handle.'

'She is not!' Kim glared at him, indignant. (Kim really *was* a gawker.) 'Skinny's horrible, it's when you haven't got any shape — and who was that beastly boy you were with the other night?'

'What beastly boy?' said Mrs Carr.

'That *Steven*.'

'He's my room mate,' said Jamie, 'and he isn't beastly.'

'Yes, he is . . . all superior. Thinking he's *funny*. Well, he's not — at least, *I* don't think so.'

'What you think or don't think,' said Jamie, 'is of the utmost irrelevance.'

Kim stuck out her tongue.

'Now you're talking like him — *trying* to talk like him. Only you can't, because you haven't got the same lardy dardy sort of voice. When you do it it just sounds *stupid*.'

There were times, thought Jamie, when Kim could be every bit as trying as Steven.

*   *   *

Anita, when he turned up as ordered at one o'clock, seemed subdued — unsure how to treat him, as if at any moment he might turn on her and bite. After her exhibition of last Saturday, he was not surprised. Since he himself, however, was also treading warily, no longer certain just where he stood, it was as well that Mummy and Daddy were there: without them, the conversation would have been decidedly sticky. Fortunately, he and Daddy were on familiar terms by now. They didn't have a great deal in common, since Jamie knew nothing whatsoever about being a sales director and Daddy knew very little more about training for the ballet, but in spite of that they had developed their own brand of what Anita had once, in somewhat contemptuous tones, called 'masculine bonhomie', which meant that Daddy quite often winked at Jamie over Anita's head, or grinned at him, knowingly, man-to-man, or applied to him for support in moments of crisis when Mummy and Anita had ganged up against him. Today, as they were tackling their starters (half an avocado pear with some sort of yellowy sauce poured in it) he said: 'So how is the world treating you, young man? Well, I trust?'

'You know it is,' said Mummy. 'We told you . . . he passed his audition.'

'Ah!' Daddy nodded. 'Of course; I was forgetting. I take it congratulations are in order?'

'That's the very reason we invited him to lunch,' said Mummy.

'Is it? I hadn't realized. I thought we were just being sociable.'

Daddy beamed, amiably. Jamie, having waited a moment to be certain, selected the smaller of his spoons and dug it into the avocado.

'Well, well! There you are. One lives and learns.' Daddy was obviously in one of his talkative moods. 'And how are you getting on,' he said, 'with all the little dolly birds? Now that you have a place of your own . . . leading the life of O'Reilly, I'll be bound!'

'He doesn't have little dolly birds any more,' said Anita. 'He's given them up.'

With his mouth full of avocado, Jamie froze. He didn't care for the way she'd said that.

'Given them up?' echoed Daddy. 'At his age?'

'Yes.' Anita smiled, and with that air of cool poise which she could sometimes assume hooked her hair back over her ears. She looked at Jamie, challengingly, across the table. 'He has boy friends now, instead.'

There was a moment of silence. Jamie swallowed a mouthful of avocado and made an unwelcome discovery: avocado pear tasted like soap. He wondered how he was going to get through the rest of it.

'*A* boy friend,' said Anita, 'anyway.'

It was Mummy and Daddy he mainly felt sorry for. They hadn't been to Tenterden Comprehensive, doing battle with the philistines; they probably weren't accustomed to people throwing out that sort of remark at their own dinner table. Anita really ought to have known better. Furthermore, he didn't understand why she had said it. On purpose, presumably, to embarrass him — but why should she want to? In any case, it had misfired. All she had succeeded in doing was embarrassing her parents.

'Really,' said Mummy, trying valiantly to pretend that it hadn't happened, 'I don't know *what* Mrs A. has done with this vinaigrette. It's far too oily — don't you find it so?'

She addressed the question to the table in general. Daddy made a vague agreeing noise at the back of his throat: Anita, punch drunk on her own little burst of malice, ignored it.

'I've never had an avocado before,' said Jamie. If no one else was going to come to the rescue, then obviously he would have to do so. 'I've seen them in the shops, and on menus and things, but I've never actually had one.'

Mummy latched on to it, gratefully.

'Haven't you?' she said. 'I do hope you like it.'

'It's a bit sort of . . . soapy,' he said.

'Soapy!' Anita gave a superior snicker of amusement. Mummy looked at her, sharply.

'The first time you had one you were sick all over the place.'

'That was when I was *ten*.'

'It's still an acquired taste, whatever your age. Don't eat it if you don't like it, Jamie.'

'I might as well give it a bash,' he said. 'Might grow into it.'

Anita watched him, across the table.

'I'd have thought everyone had tasted avocado.'

'*I*'d have thought everyone knew what a Châteaubriand was,' said Daddy. 'It just shows how wrong you can be. Would you believe —' he turned to Jamie: one man of the world to another —

'would you believe that only a few weeks ago she was under the impression it was something to drink? A kind of red wine, if I'm not much mistaken.'

Anita flushed, angrily. Obviously, thought Jamie, whatever a château-whatever-it-was was, it wasn't wine. (If anyone had asked him, on a quiz show or anything, it was what he'd have plumped for.)

'I knew perfectly well it was steak! That was just a momentary slip.'

'Many things are,' said Daddy. 'On the whole, it does not do to refine too much upon them. Nor to draw attention to them in public — not unless one wants a taste of one's own medicine. If I were you, young lady, I should remember that for the future — Jamie, why don't you give that pear up as a bad job? I must say I've always found them grossly overrated. Let me pour you some liquid refreshment — take the taste away.'

Anita spent the rest of the meal in a sulk. He couldn't understand what her problem was, other than the fact that she had been made to look small, which evidently she didn't like, but she could hardly blame him for that. She was the one who had started it: *he* hadn't even retaliated. He would have liked to tackle her about it afterwards, but she made very sure he didn't get the chance. Wherever Mummy went, Anita went too ('*I*'ll help take the dishes down, *I*'ll help bring the coffee up') flying out of the room like a startled pony the minute there seemed the least danger of their being left alone together. Going home in the car she insisted Jamie sit in the front with Daddy, so that they could 'talk motor-cars together': her own contribution was practically nil.

'I'll give you a ring,' said Jamie, as he got out at Hammersmith.

Anita shrugged her shoulders. She didn't actually say 'suit yourself', but it was plain that that was what she meant.

He telephoned her on Monday evening, after class.

'When can I see you?'

There was a silence; then: 'When did you want to see me?'

'Any time that suits you . . . soon as possible.'

More silence.

'What d'you want to see me *for*?'

Exasperated, he said: 'Do I have to have a specific reason?' This was like fixing an appointment with the dentist. 'Maybe I just want to see you because I just want to see you.'

'That would make a change,' said Anita.

He held the handset away from him and looked at it, reproachfully. What had he done to deserve that?

'I suppose I could see you tomorrow evening,' she said. She said it in the grudging tones of one who is prepared to bestow precisely five minutes of her precious time and not a second more.

'I'll come round and pick you up,' said Jamie.

'Pick me up? Why? Where are we going?'

'Go and have a coffee somewhere.' He'd just received his pay cheque. He could afford, if he wanted, to stand her something to eat. 'Go to McDonald's,' he said.

'I don't like McDonald's.'

She didn't like McDonald's. — *Why* didn't she like McDonald's? As a matter of principle, that was why. She wouldn't like anywhere if he were the one to suggest it.

'All right, then,' he said. 'You think of somewhere.'

'We could go to the Vegeburger.'

'OK. We'll go to the Vegeburger.' He didn't care where they went, so long as they went somewhere. 'I'll come round directly after class.'

The Vegeburger served burgers filled with onions and spun protein.

'I'm thinking of turning vegetarian,' said Anita.

'Oh, yes?' At any other time such a statement might have interested him; tonight it did not. He listened with half an ear while she extolled the health-giving properties of beans and lentils, then, seizing the opportunity of a brief break in the monologue, dived straight in with: 'So what were all the snide remarks in aid of the other day?'

'Snide remarks?' She did her best to look wide-eyed and innocent. 'What snide remarks?'

'All that about me having boy friends.'

He didn't bother to keep his voice down. A couple of heads on the far side of the room turned, covertly, to look at him: he noted with malicious satisfaction the tide of pink wash over Anita's cheeks.

'You don't have to yell,' she said.

'Why? Isn't it the sort of thing you like people to hear?'

'I wouldn't have thought it was the sort of thing *you'd* like people to hear.'

'I suppose that's why you said it?'

There was a pause. Anita, with elaborate interest, investigated her vegeburger.

'It's no different from how it was two seconds ago,' said Jamie. 'Why don't you answer my question?'

'I've forgotten what it was.'

'I asked you, what was with all the snide remarks?'

'They weren't snide.'

'Oh? So what would you call them?'

'They were just observations. Part of the conversation.'

'Ordinary, everyday, polite conversation?'

'Yes. Well —' She looked up at him, a hint of defiance in her green eyes. 'It's true, isn't it?'

'What is?'

'You and Steven.'

'What about me and Steven?'

'Well —'

Her voice petered out.

'Is that what you really believe?' he said. 'I mean, if it *is* what you really believe —' If it was what she really believed, then he might as well give up. He might just as well have let Steven have what he wanted and be done with it. At least he'd have been making *some*one happy. 'There's no flaming justice in this world, is there?' he said.

Anita kept her gaze fixed firmly on the remains of her vegeburger.

'I'm sorry.'

It was a bit late in the day for being sorry; the damage had already been done. His only hope was that Mummy was not the gossiping sort. His dad would go raving berserk. He looked frowningly at Anita, as she sat there, earnestly studying the composition of her vegeburger.

'It still doesn't explain why you went and said it. I mean —' He swept his hair back out of his eyes. 'I mean, *Jesus* . . . in front of your *parents*.'

Anita swallowed.

'I'm sorry,' she said.

It was the second time she'd said it. It still didn't explain.

'I mean, even if you *did* believe it . . . why'd you have to go and *say* it?'

She humped a shoulder.

'Don't know. S'pose I was feeling mean.'

Mean? Why should she feel mean, for God's sake? What was he supposed to have done?

'It wasn't because of that thing with Doreen, was it? Getting engaged, and all? Because if it was, I told you . . . it was a misunderstanding.'

'It wasn't that.'

'Then what was it?'

She took a breath.

'You and Steven. At the party.'

Him and *Steven*? What about her and the Gawker?

'We didn't do anything at the party.' Apart from Steven being facetious and showing off, and that was hardly Jamie's fault. *He* wasn't responsible for the way other people chose to behave.

196

'Anyway,' he said, 'what about you and that Gawker?'

She looked up, puzzled.

'What gawker?'

'Old Martin Redleg, or whatever his name is.'

'Oh! Martin.' That had made her uncomfortable. *As well it might.* 'Martin doesn't mean anything.'

He resisted the temptation to retort that no one would have guessed as much from her behaviour.

'Neither does Steven,' he said.

Anita pursed her lips.

'Well, he doesn't,' said Jamie. 'You've just got a thing against him.'

'I haven't got a thing against him! I don't like him, that's all. I don't know what you see in him . . . he makes me squirm.'

'He doesn't make most girls squirm. Most girls go for him in a big way.' Kim hadn't, of course; but then Kim was unaccountable. 'Most girls think he's attractive.'

'Then most girls must be raving potty. Martin says —' She stopped; aware, too late, of her mistake.

'What does Martin say?'

She tilted her head.

'Martin says he wouldn't know what to do with a girl if he got one.'

'You mean *Martin* wouldn't . . . great gawker.'

'What exactly,' said Anita, sidetracked, '*is* a gawker?'

'A prat,' said Jamie. 'Otherwise known as an arseole.'

'I thought it might be.' She giggled; Jamie grinned. 'I'll tell you who *is* a gawker . . . ghastly Gover. Does it apply to women?'

'Applies to anyone,' said Jamie. He didn't tell her it was one of Steven's words. He felt, instinctively, that it would not be wise. 'Martin Redleg, ghastly Gover . . . anyone you care to name. Feel like another coffee?'

The coffees came, along with two more vegeburgers, which he had decided were quite palatable.

'Not bad, this hand-knitted stuff . . . tastes almost like the real thing. I guess when you come to think of it, there isn't any need for people to go round gorging flesh. I guess you could exist just as well on beans and things.'

He said it in the hope of pleasing her, but it was her mind, now, that was obviously not on the subject. Quite suddenly, as he was in the middle of telling her about an aunt of his who had existed for twenty years on nothing but watercress, she said: 'I've been offered a share in a flat for next term.'

'Oh?'

'One of the girls is moving out — Marcia Webley. She's going to join a company in Paris. They've asked me if I'd like to take her place.'

'And are you going to?'

'I think so; if Mummy and Daddy agree. They said they'd talk about it and let me know . . . it's mixed, you see.'

'*Mixed?*'

'The flat — four boys and two girls.'

'Some flat!'

'Yes, it's huge. The whole ground floor. You have to share bedrooms, of course, but I don't mind that. Actually —' She hesitated. 'Actually, one of the boys is moving out as well. I *was* going to ask if you'd like to take his place, but —'

'But what?'

'I suppose you won't want to, now.'

What did she mean, *now*?

'Now that you're both going to be full-time ... I suppose you'll want to stick together.'

For crying out *loud*.

'We're not Siamese flaming twins!' Just because they happened to share a room, it didn't mean they were married, for God's sake.

'But won't he mind?' said Anita.

'Too bad if he does.' They had made no vows of eternal friendship. 'Where is the flat, anyway?'

'Holland Park — quite easy for Ealing.'

Not that it mattered. He wouldn't have cared if it were South Wimbledon: if Anita were going to be there, then so was he.

'I'll come,' he said.

Still she seemed doubtful.

'Well? What's the matter? Don't you *want* me to come?'

'Yes, of course! I wouldn't have asked you otherwise.'

'So?'

'I just have this awful feeling,' she said, 'that he'll talk you out of it.'

He would not talk him out of it: he had made up his mind. What was it about him that made everyone think he could be so easily swayed?

10

He arrived back in Hammersmith to find Steven
laying out a row of newly washed socks and
underpants on the window ledge to dry. Taking
the bull by the horns, he said: 'I've been offered a
share in a flat for next term.'

'Really?' said Steven.

'Yeah ... with Anita and some others. I'm
seriously thinking about taking it.'

He braced himself, waiting for the storm that
would surely break. Instead, scarcely pausing in
his laying out of underpants, Steven said: 'If I
were you I should stop thinking and start acting
... snap it up before some other bugger leaps in.'

He could hardly believe that he was hearing
correctly. These past couple of weeks, Steven had
shown definite and disturbing tendencies
towards possessiveness. It had been, *Where are
you going*? and *What are you doing*? and *When
are you likely to be in*? A scene of some kind had
seemed inevitable.

'It doesn't bother you?' he said. He felt
relieved, naturally — but perhaps not quite so
gratified as he might have done. He would have

expected *some* kind of reaction; then he would have explained that it was only because it was Anita, and that if it had been anyone else he would have said no, but seeing as it was her, and she was the one he had to thank for being at Kendra Hall in the first place, it did rather put him under an obligation, so that he didn't very well see how he could get out of it, and —

'As a matter of fact,' said Steven, 'it solves a problem . . . I'd thought of giving this place up in any case.'

'*Oh*?' That was something he hadn't expected. 'And go where?'

'Somewhere a bit more upmarket. Somewhere —' Steven closed the windows on his row of socks and underpants, securing them against sudden droppage into the street, two floors below. 'Somewhere, preferably, with a washing machine.'

'On a grant? You'll be lucky!'

'I'm not going to be on a grant. I decided, yesterday . . . I'm going to chuck it.'

'Chuck what?'

'This dancing lark.'

'You can't mean it?'

'I do mean it.' Calmly, Steven walked across to the mantelshelf and helped himself to a cigarette from a packet of Gauloises that was lying there. This was very strange, thought Jamie: he had never known Steven smoke before. 'Want one?'

'You must be joking!'

'Well, all right, you don't have to go all sanctimonious. I'm quite well aware of the health hazards, thank you very much. I don't need you preaching at me. If I choose to kill myself by slow degrees, that's up to me. Right?'

'Sure,' said Jamie. 'Go ahead, be my guest . . . pollute the atmosphere. Why not?'

'Why not?' agreed Steven. 'It needn't worry you — you won't be here long enough for it to kill you.'

He lit the cigarette and tossed the dead match into the hearth. Jamie noticed that there were several others already lying there.

'What's brought all this on?' he said. 'Smoking? Chucking the ballet?'

'Oh! Oh! the *ballay* . . . they've even got you at it now.'

'Don't split hairs.' He didn't believe that he *had* said the ballay: it wouldn't be in the least like him. 'What was the point of bothering to take an audition if you didn't intend to go ahead?'

'Didn't know at that time, did I? Only just made my mind up. It's like I told you, right at the beginning . . . I don't believe in tying myself down. Take life as it comes, that's my philosophy.'

'So what are you going to do?'

'My son —' Steven laid a finger against the side of his nose — 'I am a man of many parts . . . who knows what I might not do? Start up a business? Found an empire? — might even go back into movies.'

'Yeah — blue movies!' He'd put two and two together by now. He might be a bit slow, but he wasn't completely thick.

Steven smiled; unruffled.

'So it's a way of earning a living.'

'Some living!'

'There are those,' murmured Steven, 'who would say that about the ballet ... can you honestly contemplate the sheer and utter boredom of doing those bloody awful barre exercises for the rest of your working life?'

Jamie shrugged. The prospect didn't particularly bother him.

'Well, there you are,' said Steven. 'Some of us can, some of us can't. I happen to be one of those that can't. And even if I could —' he drew on his cigarette, looking pensively for a second or so at the glowing tip — 'even if I could, I don't believe in getting too bound up in relationships. I like to move around; play the field. Talking of which, do I take it that you have finally decided to give up chasing every female within sight and settle for the one that's been there under your nose from the word go?'

He stiffened; automatically preparing to be on his guard. He resented Steven interfering in matters which were no concern of his.

'If you mean Anita —'

'Who else? I told you, didn't I,' said Steven, 'that you were wasting your time trying to knock off all the rest of the rubbish when there was quality goods just lying around for the taking? Beats me why you didn't get stuck in there ages ago — she's only flesh and blood, when all's said and done. Why do you think she put on that floor show the other night with the Gawker?'

He still found that something of a puzzle —

she'd said herself that the Gawker didn't mean anything to her. Coldly, he shook his head.

'I haven't the least idea.'

'Don't be a cretin! She did it for your benefit, didn't she? With the intention, you buffoon, of rousing your masculine instincts.'

Jamie looked at him.

'Honestly,' said Steven, 'you wouldn't win any prizes in the quick-off-the-draw stakes, would you? Dozy great yum yum! She makes it just about as plain as a girl can, short of actually coming up and asking for it, and all old Dopy can do is shake his head and look gormless. What do you want? You want it spelt out in words of one syllable? She-wants-you? She-fancies-'

'Fancies,' said Jamie, 'is two syllables.'

'All right! So you've spotted today's deliberate mistake! Give yourself a gold star and a pat on the back. You know what your trouble is? You walk around with your eyes shut, that's what your trouble is.'

'Yeah, and you know what yours is, don't you?' retorted Jamie. 'Can't resist shooting your mouth off about matters of which you are dead ignorant.'

Steven grinned.

'Not *dead* ignorant?'

'Well, put it this way . . . there are times when you don't flaming well know what you're talking about.'

'In this case, however, my son, you may rest assured that I do. Human psychology is my strong point. When it comes to people, I am very rarely wrong.'

'Oh, no?' said Jamie.

'Well, I'll admit I dropped a bit of a clanger where you were concerned, but that was understandable: my passions were roused. I was in no fit state to think clearly. When my emotions are not involved I'm like a human calculating machine ... By the way —' Steven stubbed out his cigarette in half a cup of cold coffee — 'I'm going to be out Friday evening. Just thought you'd like to know.'

He agonized long and hard before finally telephoning Anita and inviting her round for dinner. Even if what Steven had said were true (and grudgingly it had to be admitted that he did *some* times seem to know what he was talking about) he still couldn't bring himself to approach Anita in quite the same cavalier spirit as he would Pauline or Kate. Pauline or Kate could take pot luck: for Anita a special effort had to be made. (He remembered that on the only previous occasion she had come round he had purposely, as an act of defiance, left the bed unmade and the floor strewn with clothes. He blushed, now, for his own uncouthness.)

On Friday, in his lunch break, he went shopping in the store.

'And what 'ave we 'ere?' said Dennis, as he arrived back in the basement selfconsciously carrying a Plumber's plastic carrier bag. '*Candles*, already?' (Dennis was no respecter of other people's property. He worked on the basis of 'What's mine is mine and what's yours is everybody else's.') 'Paper *serviettes* — bottle o' *vino*? Are you by any chance hentertaining royalty?'

He could hardly have gone to any more pains. Immediately on his return from work he tidied up the room, making Steven's bed as well as his own, thrusting odd garments, willy nilly, out of sight into the first drawer or cupboard that came to hand, removing the dust of ages from window ledges and mantelshelf with the help of an old pair of socks. After tidying the room he had a quick shower in the communal bathroom on the first floor, dressed himself in clean clothes (having been home the previous weekend, he fortunately had some) and spent five minutes in front of the mirror combing his hair, an operation he was not normally much given to bothering with. He toyed with the idea, as he was doing it, of borrowing Steven's razor and scraping off what had by now become an unmistakable shadow, but finally deciding against it (on the grounds that perchance by candlelight it might look distinguished) he turned his attention instead to the laying of the table.

The table was small and rickety, with a yellow plastic top, and it bothered him that he had no cloth to cover it with. Mummy and Daddy admittedly never covered theirs with a cloth, but then theirs was not yellow plastic. In the end he hit upon a bright idea: at the bottom of one of the drawers in the old Victorian sideboard which did duty as a clothes cupboard was some pink lining paper. He extracted it, smoothed it out, spread it over the table and secured it underneath with strips of Sellotape. On top he laid a couple of table mats which he had filched from the hall table downstairs (they had large circular marks where pot plants had stood on them, but with the light out it would never show); two of his paper serviettes, folded triangularly; their one and only wine goblet, for Anita; the toothglass, for himself; and a varied selection of battered cutlery — all the cutlery was twisted into odd shapes, as if former occupants of the room had either spent their time spoon-bending or opening tins of sardines. In the centre of the table he stuck a candle in an old cider bottle which he had found in the dustbin: the other candles he stood about the room in saucers. When they were all alight the effect was quite artistic — quite Bohemian. Like something out of the Hunchback's trendy French movie which he had insisted they all watch. There was even a faint aroma of genuine French cigarette smoke from Steven's French cigarettes. Gauloises, or whatever they had been. (Trust Steven to smoke *French* cigarettes. He ought to get together with the Hunchback, they'd probably go down a treat with each other.)

He had told Anita to get there for eight o'clock. At half past seven he switched on the oven part of the Baby Belling, which in fact was the only part which still functioned, and went down the road to fetch dinner. It hadn't been easy, deciding what to buy. Obviously it had to be something that was a cut above fish and chips, but there wasn't any point in trying to compete with artichokes or avocados. He'd decided against Greek or Turkish, on the grounds that they were an unknown quantity, hesitated over Indian, finally settled, after much thought, for Chinese; and just to show that he not only listened to what she said but actually took note of it he ordered nothing but vegetable dishes and rice. They plainly thought he was mad (mad or stingy; one or the other) but they came up with the goods: he trotted back home with a selection of five different vegetable dishes and a couple of egg fried rice, remembering, on the way, to stop off at the delicatessen for a bottle of Soya Sauce for flavouring and a tin of lychees for afterwards.

Anita arrived precisely on the dot of eight o'clock. She was wearing the little white dress she had worn at the party and had her hair hanging loose about her shoulders. She'd taken to doing it that way quite a lot just lately: he couldn't help wondering if by any chance the Gawker had expressed a liking for it.

He led her upstairs to his candlelit cavern. Gratifyingly, the first thing she said as they entered was 'Jamie, how super! It's like a bistro!' She even noticed that it smelt like one.

'Yeah,' he said. 'French fags. Must have drifted up from downstairs.'

He didn't tell her that they had Steven's Gauloises to thank; he reckoned the less said about Steven the better. As it happened, it was Anita herself who mentioned him.

'Is Steven out?' she said. She said it cautiously, as if half expecting he might be hiding somewhere in a cupboard. 'Or is he —'

'Out,' said Jamie. 'Feel like some music?'

He sorted through the records in search of something suitable. There wasn't very much. Johnny Martyr was plainly out of the question, and so was the concrete stuff. No one wanted concrete music with Chinese food.

'D'you care for The Who?'

It seemed that The Who were one of her favourites. The wine he had chosen, which he had bought principally because it was on offer, was also one of her favourites, but Indian food, on the other hand, she didn't much care for, so that it was just as well he had plumped for Chinese.

'And nothing but vegetables,' he said, anxious for approval.

'Yes, and you see —' she gazed at him, earnestly, across the table —' one doesn't actually *miss* not having meat, does one? I mean, if you didn't know you wouldn't have noticed. Or would you, do you think?'

At that moment he wouldn't have noticed what he was eating. It had just come to his attention that under the little white dress, all openwork and lacy, she wasn't wearing any bra. Not that she really needed one — or at least, not for the purposes of control. At the same time, no one could have called her flat-chested. Definitely not.

'*Would* you?' said Anita.

'Would I —?' For just a second, such was the state of his mind, he thought she was putting to him the question that Doug so often used to put, ogling after some passing female: '*I* would . . .

would you?' Then he realized. 'Oh!' he said. 'No. No, I don't expect I would.'

'That's what I keep telling Auntie Margaret. She keeps trying to force pork chops and things down me, and I keep telling her . . . it's not necessary. You don't need it.'

'That's right,' said Jamie. 'You don't.' He wondered if *she* would, if he were to ask her. Even now, he couldn't bring himself to think of her the same way he did Pauline and Sharon and the rest of them. All very well Steven saying she was only flesh and blood, but there was flesh and blood and there was flesh and blood. Anita just wasn't the same as all the others.

'You can get all the protein you need,' she was saying, 'out of vegetables.'

'But then, of course,' said Jamie, 'man cannot live by the potato alone.'

She stared at him.

'I'm not suggesting one lives on potatoes.'

'Ah. That's all right, then. I mean —'

What *did* he mean?

He knew what he meant; it was just a question of finding the words to put it in.

'I mean . . . there are other things in life.'

'Oh, I agree,' said Anita. 'Eating's only a functional necessity.'

That wasn't what he had meant.

'If I had my way,' said Anita, 'we'd all live on pills. Then we wouldn't have to bother sitting down to meals at all.'

This wasn't very promising. He obviously wasn't expressing himself forcibly enough.

210

'What I mean —' He pushed his hair back out of his eyes, giving himself time to think. 'What I mean is, there's still a lot of the beast in us.'

'Oh, well, of course! But that's what civilization's all about, isn't it? Suppressing mere animal instincts in favour of more humanized ones.'

'Except we can't suppress them *all*,' he said. 'Otherwise humanity would just come to a full stop.' Unless she wanted to start doing it entirely by test tubes. But then, if that were the case, she surely wouldn't be wearing a little white dress full of holes without any bra underneath? He cheered up. 'Have some lychees,' he said. 'Out of a tin . . . can't get more civilized than that.'

Actually, as he quickly discovered, you could: it helped if you had a tin opener. He went upstairs to borrow one from Miss Mincing, who lived in the attics and sold secrets to the Russians (at least, that was Jamie's theory: Steven said she was a prostitute). When he came back, Anita was kneeling on the floor by the record player, looking at the Johnny Martyr record.

'I don't think you'd like that one,' he said.

'Why not?'

'I just don't think you would.' It wasn't the sort of atmosphere he wanted to create: it didn't go with the candlelight and the French cigarette smoke. Firmly, he took it away from her. What was needed was something beautiful and romantic, but knowing Steven that was probably too much to hope for.

'Let's have this one,' said Anita.

He peered at it.

'Tchaikvosky's Sixth Symphony?'

With misgivings, he put it on. He still had unhappy memories, from school, of being forced to listen to Beethoven, until, at the age of thirteen, they'd finally decided he was a musical cretin and had relegated him to the metalwork class, where he'd been even more of a cretin.

'Is it any good?' he said.

'It's gorgeous,' said Anita. 'Honestly ... I could die to it.'

He didn't want her to die to it, he wanted her to get turned on by it. He didn't see how anyone could get turned on by a symphony.

'D'you want to come and sit on the bed?' he said. 'It's more comfortable there.'

'All right,' said Anita.

They sat together, side by side, bolt upright, feet on the floor, carefully not touching. Jamie was aware of Anita's hand, on the bed, within centimetres of his own. If he just stretched out a finger . . .

It took him a while to nerve himself: stretching out a finger had become, of a sudden, an act of the deepest significance. If she moved away, he would know that Steven had been wrong. Contrariwise, if she moved *closer* —

She didn't move closer, but neither, on the other hand, did she move away. They sat rigid, through the whole of the first side of Tchaikovsky's Sixth Symphony, the tips of their fingers just barely touching. If anyone had told him, before this, that simply touching the tips of a

212

girl's fingers could do things to you he'd have said they must be kinky.

The side came to an end and he crawled across the floor on hands and knees to turn the record over. In normal circumstances he would have been appalled at the thought of having to sit in silence through all four movements of someone's symphony. This evening, four movements seemed scarcely long enough.

When he returned to the bed he found that Anita had kicked off her shoes and was sitting curled up against the wall, her feet tucked beneath her. He humped himself across to sit with her. This time they sat with not only the tips of their fingers touching but with their actual bodies glued together, all the way down from the shoulders to the hips. He was tinglingly aware of the closeness of her. His skin, encased in its statutory layers of clothing, had acquired a new sensitivity, to which even the coarseness of blue denim was no bar: the pressure of Anita's knee against his set off a series of sparks that went shooting in a chain reaction throughout his body like a myriad tiny jets of flame.

Experimentally, he slipped an arm about her. For a second she stiffened, and he thought she was going to move; but then, awkwardly, with none of the grace or fluidity she normally showed, she leaned her head against his shoulder.

They sat for a few moments, posed and unyielding, like a piece of ornamental statuary. This is most uncomfortable, thought Jamie.

My arm is going dead.

My neck is getting a crick.

I must *do* something.

With his free hand, he tipped her face up towards him and pressed his lips firmly against hers.

This was it: the moment of truth.

*Ja*mie!
Don't.
DO YOU MIND?
WHAM!

Except that by the law of averages, everyone had to have a lucky break sooner or later.

Or perhaps it wasn't so much a lucky break as managing at last to find the right person — with a little help from Steven, it had to be admitted. All right, so he didn't mind admitting it. He wasn't proud. So he had Steven to thank. So what? He could afford to be generous — now.

From somewhere or other he heard a voice.

His voice.

It seemed to be speaking of its own volition.

'I love you,' it was saying. 'I love you.'

It sounded incredibly corny; like something out of some junk TV soap opear. But still it kept on saying it.

'I love you, I love you . . .'

Anita wrapped both arms round his neck.

'I love you too,' she whispered.

Somehow, it didn't sound quite so corny coming from her. In fact, it didn't sound corny at all. He would have liked to hear more of it, but instead, to his indignation and disgust, what he heard were the unmistakable sound of footsteps creaking on the floorboards outside, followed by the equally unmistakable sounds of a key being inserted in the lock. Anita raised her head from the pillow.

'What's that?'

'Don't worry.' Grim-faced, Jamie swung himself off the bed. 'Whatever it is, it's not coming in.'

He yanked open the door mere seconds ahead of Steven. Steven looked surprised.

'Oh! — Great. Thanks.'

'Don't thank me,' said Jamie.

'What?'

'I said, don't thank me.'

'Why? What are you —'

'Down,' said Jamie.

'Down?'

'Down!' He pointed, in a fury, at the stairs. Steven, after a momentary hesitation, began slowly and protestingly to descend. He went down backwards, one step at a time, keeping a wary eye upon Jamie as he did so.

'What are you playing at?'

'I might ask you the same question! What are you doing here?'

'What do you mean, what am I doing here? I live here!'

'Don't try being smart with me! I thought you said you were going to be out?'

'Well, I've been out, haven't I? Now I've come back.'

'At half past nine at night?'

'Yes. Well —' Steven reached the first landing

and carefully negotiated the curve. He was still going backwards, still keeping one eye fixed nervously on Jamie. 'Things didn't work out.'

'Too bad!'

'So what am I supposed to do? Tramp the streets for the next couple of hours?'

'Why not?'

'Come off it!' said Steven. 'It's raining cats and dogs out there.'

'So go and sit in the pub. See what trade you can pick up.'

'Look —' Steven missed the last step, snatched too late at the banister rail and ricocheted backwards into the hall. 'This is my room you're turning me out of.'

'Our room,' said Jamie. 'And I happen to be in possession of it, so you can just shove off . . . go on!' He took the last few stairs at a bound, grabbed Steven by the collar and forcibly manhandled him to the front door. 'Shove!'

'But look at it!' said Steven.

Jamie looked. It was, indeed, coming down in buckets.

'You can't do this to me!'

At any other time, he probably couldn't. Tonight, he could. He held open the door.

'Out!'

Steven whimpered. He turned up his coat collar.

'Have you no heart?'

'Yes, but just at this moment it happens to be otherwise engaged . . . go on!' He gave him a push. 'Get going!'

'I'll remember this,' said Steven. 'I'll get even with you, don't you worry!'

'Tell us about it later,' said Jamie.

He closed the door and turned back, into the hall. From the second floor, the strains of Tchaikovsky's Sixth Symphony could be heard. He set off, three at a time, up the stairs. He couldn't waste precious minutes bandying words with Steven, he had other matters on his mind.

He had just made an important discovery: he was in love . . .

THE END

ZAK
by Frances Thomas

Life at William Wordsworth School is dull, dull,
dull – at least that's what Mark Sullivan thinks.
But then one day Zak walks into Form IVF's
Biology lesson and nothing is quite the same
again. For Zak is unlike anyone Mark ever met
before. Tall, suntanned and very rich, he attracts
the girls like a magnet, and it is even rumoured
that his father is a megastar. But there's a
strange mystery surrounding him – just who
exactly *is* Zak?

0 552 523623

**FREEWAY – REAL VARIETY AND SPICE
FOR OLDER READERS**

THE STALKER
by Joan Lowery Nixon

Bobbie Trax's mother has been murdered — strangled, the police say, by her own daughter. But Jennifer Wilcox, Bobbie's closest friend, knows she is innocent — and will do anything to prove it.

With an unfolding trail of clues, Jennifer's task seems hopeless — until she teams up with ex-detective Lucas Maldonaldo. Together they search for a vicious killer. But Jennifer is being watched. Someone is stalking her. Suddenly the hunter has become the hunted.

0 552 523690

FREEWAY — REAL VARIETY AND SPICE FOR OLDER READERS

TIME ROPE
by Robert Leeson

They were strangers when they met under the tree with its mysterious hanging rope. But when Tod, Fee and Roller each takes a swing on the rope they are transported, fifty, one hundred, two hundred years into the past, to the blood and heat of battlefields in Spain, to the passions and treacheries of Regency England, to the brutal sufferings of chain gangs in the Caribbean forests. Their fates mysteriously linked – with each other and with the enigmatic time research underway in the futuristic world of 2034 to which they will eventually travel, the three must discover exactly who and what they will be – in their own future.

A startlingly original quartet of novels from this well-known author.

Future titles:
2: THREE AGAINST THE WORLD
3: AT WAR WITH TOMORROW
4: THE METRO GANGS ATTACK

FREEWAY – REAL VARIETY AND SPICE FOR OLDER READERS

PLEASE DON'T GO
by Peggy Woodford

She's fifteen, in France, and in love for the first time ever!

Mary is on an exchange student trip to France and she is enchanted by everything she finds — the place, the way of life, the food, the smells and especially the people. During this unforgettable summer, she meets Antoine — handsome, married Antoine who is more than twice her age and is the first man ever to kiss her. And she also meets Joël — tall, gangly red-haired Joël who seems to want to be more than a friend . . .

0 552 524573

FREEWAY – REAL VARIETY AND SPICE FOR OLDER READERS